All about the
Great Dane

The author with Bessie
Braddock.

All about the Great Dane

Bruce MacDonald

PELHAM BOOKS

First published in Great Britain by
PELHAM BOOKS LTD
27 Wrights Lane
London W8 5TZ
1987
Reprinted 1988

British Library Cataloguing in Publication Data

Macdonald, Bruce
    All about the Great Dane.—(All about)
    1. Great Danes
    I. Title   II. Series
    636.7′3   SF429.G7

ISBN 0 7207 1724 8

Typeset by Sunrise Setting, Torquay
Printed and bound by Butler & Tanner, Frome

This book is dedicated with love to my partner Maggie Down, whose inspiration it was and whose nagging made me write it all down, and to our dogs and cats, Great Aunt Sally, Bessie Braddock, Officer Dibble, Jampot, Charlotte, Smartie, Pansy Potter, Angel, Fella, Dizie, Blaster, Scrummy, Foggy, Artè, Polo, Spook and Teka who did their level best to hinder me; to Frank Lloyd-Griffiths and Mark Furber, our vets for many years, for their unfailing kindness and compassion.

Contents

Acknowledgements

The author acknowledges with grateful thanks the following:
MAGGIE DOWN for her countless hours of support, work and photographs.
CANDY BATCHELOR for her superb line drawings.
NELLIE ENNALS for making sure I got the history right.
JOYCE WRIGHT for her charming poems.
GINA BOWERS for helping with the list of champions.
JANET SILVESTER for the final typing.

Many breeders and owners for photographs, especially RON LEWIS.

Professional Photographers:
Sally Ann Thompson, Diane Pearce, Roger Chambers, Dave Freeman, Thomas Fall, David Dalton, Alan V. Walker, Gerald Foyle, Michael M. Trafford, Derek Davis, John Hopwood, King's and others.

The Kennel Club, the American Kennel Club and the Deutscher Doggen Club for permission to reproduce their respective Great Dane Breed Standards.

Just Beautiful!

So you want a Great Dane puppy.
Will you want it all its life?
Will it be 'all important', like
family and wife?

Will you handle it with gentleness
and pat it when it's good?
And see its water's always fresh
and that it's got good food?

Will you train it kindly?
And brush it every day?
And provide it with a clean dry bed
where it can go and lay?

Will you teach the children
that they too must be kind?
And if the puppy takes their toys
they really mustn't mind.

Will you train it on the lead
to sit, and walk to heel?
Not drag it on a choke-chain
with all the pain to feel.

Will you teach obedience?
To come, when it's afar.
To lay and stay if needed,
and be good in the car.

And when it's learnt these lessons,
and loves you all so true,
will you thank the day this Great Dane
came to live with you?

And when it's old and feeble,
and life has passed it by,
your family broken-hearted
and not an eye is dry,

Will you still be happy
that you bought that puppy Dane?
And will you get another
and start it all again?

If you can answer 'Yes' my friend
to all that I have said,
then you deserve a Great Dane,
the best one ever bred.

But if you've read my questions,
and cannot answer true,
please DON'T have a Great Dane:
it's not fair to him or you.

                              Joyce Wright, 1985

Author's Introduction

In 1939 I, like so many youngsters, spent much of my time in the local cinema. There was nothing very unusual about that for there was no television in my area at that time and I disliked football, and cricket was limited to the sunnier days of summer. My father was the cinema manager which meant that I could see more films than my friends. I had a definite financial advantage in that I did not have to pay for admission to the 'house of magic'. Everyone has a favourite type of film and I was no exception: in

I will soon grow into my ears.

my case it was those with animals – the lions and elephants of Tarzan, the horses of the American cowboy heroes and even the antics of Mickey Mouse and his friends, not forgetting that canny canine Pluto. During that year there were two memorable events. The first and most important to the adult population was the start of World War Two. The second was the general release of the film Version of *The Hound of The Baskervilles*, and it was after seeing the Sherlock Holmes thriller that I decided to have a Great Dane of my own one day! My parents thought it a passing fancy (they had bred Scottish Terriers for many years) but for once they were wrong.

Whilst travelling as a salesman through the Warwickshire countryside many years later, I called at a shop in the village of Rowington. The conversation, after concluding a business transaction, turned to the subject of dogs and especially to Great Danes. This was the year I would fulfil my childhood dream. The shopkeeper said, 'I think the local vicar's wife does a bit of breeding,' an understatement if ever there was one, for the local vicar's wife turned out to be Olive Davies, the wife of the Rev. Gwynn Davies with whom she owned the famous Oldmanor Kennels of Great Danes. It took numerous visits to the vicarage and much interrogation before an enchanting puppy became mine. She was Fawn with a dark mask and the impish charm that a puppy should have. Sheba and I were inseparable, she travelled with me from her first day, with picnic meals eaten in the parks of various towns and cities we visited. During the following months she developed into a beautiful young bitch and I entered her in a few local dog shows. It was at one of these shows that she insisted on placing her front feet on the shoulders of the judge and licking his face with alarming enthusiasm after being awarded a prize.

The years passed by and Sheba continued to give everything she could to me – unshakable loyalty, affection and constant companionship. She was never to have any puppies, for I believed (as I do now) that puppies should never be brought into this world without the breeder having the proper facilities for the mother and her offspring. At the age of nine, dear Sheba became blind and she had a slight heart problem but showed no sign of suffering. Two years later she was to die with her head in my arms, whilst she lay on the operating table of my veterinary surgeon. She was the victim of distension – a killer in an old dog. Many years have passed since Sheba died, and more than twenty-five years since that momentous day when, travelling through Rowington, I met that vicar's wife 'who does a bit of breeding'.

Every dog has a special place in the heart of a true dog lover, with Great Danes I fear this is more so. The greatest compliment you can give when the sad parting with your old friend becomes inevitable is to obtain another of the same breed. The new dog can never be a replacement, nothing can, but I am sure he will nestle into your affections just as your first Great Dane did.

I hope that readers of this book will enjoy its contents to the full, admire the majestic Great Danes that are illustrated and, most of all, learn *All about the Great Dane*.

1 History of the Breed

As with many breeds, the origin of the Great Dane is really a mystery and is likely to stay that way. There have been drawings of dogs found within the tombs of the ancient Pharaohs and certain schools of thought imagine these to be the earliest record of the breed. In *The Natural History of the Dog* by Richard and Alice Fiennes, the illustration of Assyrian huntsmen around the year 600BC gives the impression of early Great Danes but it is not absolute proof of their existence at that time. It is claimed that dogs appearing to be Great Danes existed in Germany, Poland, France and Russia many centuries ago. The Romans could have claimed equally that the breed was theirs by origin, but again there is no proof. We are even led to believe in the existence of the Great Dane in England all those years ago, and the Romans are alleged to have employed an official known as the Procurator Cynogie; he resided in Winchester, commonly known in those days as the City of Dogs, and it was his task to obtain specimens of what we believe to be the ancestors of the Great Dane.

If we are to believe all that we have read in the past, then the Dane-like dogs of the Saxons were used to hunt wild boar and can be seen in illustrations of fourteenth- and fifteenth-century hunting scenes. Dogs which looked like the Great Dane were the Lyme Mastiffs of the sixteenth and seventeenth centuries, and so highly thought of were these dogs that many were sent to the royalty of Europe. There is no doubt that the Lyme Mastiff resembled the Great Dane but again, authenticity cannot be guaranteed. It was not until the seventeenth century that there was any real proof of the Great Dane's existence: an engraving by Richard Blomes portrays a boar hunt in Denmark, and from the number of dogs shown and from their size and conformation, there is little doubt they were the ancestors of the Great Dane.

There are references in many works to dogs known as Alaunts, and again we are tempted to believe they were early examples of the breed. There is no end to the claims made throughout the years, and without absolute proof it would be of little interest to repeat the many published words concerning the Great Dane's origins.

What really matters is that the Great Dane is here and firmly established as a recognized breed. In Britain the Great Dane has suffered many obstacles including becoming almost extinct when a rabies outbreak occurred in the nineteenth century. Further stock was imported from Germany but the expense of quarantine severely dampened the enthusiasm for importing in large numbers. As the years went by, more admirers of the breed purchased breeding stock and numbers stabilized again. The imported German dogs had cropped ears and the practice of cropping puppies in Britain was adopted. Then a further damaging blow

Mrs MacGowan's lovely import.

was dealt to the popularity of the breed by the then Prince of Wales, later King Edward VII, who expressed his dislike of ear cropping and requested the practice should cease. The fanciers of Great Danes during that period preferred the breed to have cropped ears but did not wish to oppose the wishes of the Prince, with the result that the Great Dane fell from favour for a number of years. Fortunately time healed the blow and, even though ears were never again cropped in Britain, the popularity of the breed started to increase again. Over the centuries there is little doubt that dogs the size of the Great Dane inhabited the world, and many changes must have taken place during such a prolonged period. As in the case of so many breeds of dog, the Great Danes we know today are very different from the Danes of two hundred years ago due to the influence of breeders during that time.

About one hundred years ago German and British breeders of Great Danes became obsessed with the breed and their aim was to develop the type of dog we now know and recognize as the Great Dane. The dog had to be very large and yet graceful, strong in appearance yet gentle in temperament. It has been claimed the Great Dane is a German dog by origin but there is no evidence of this; what is evident is the German breeders' leadership in developing today's dog. So proud of the breed were the Germans that in 1880 they adopted the Great Dane as the national dog and the name *Deutsche Dogge* was chosen for this noble creature. It was unfortunate that the breed was still called by a number of different names which caused chaos, for in the same period that the *Deutsche Dogge* was established, there arrived on the scene the *Danish Doggen* and the *Ulmer Doggen*. It was most odd that the *Danish Doggen* should appear at all, for there was no record of any such dog being bred in Denmark, and according to the pedigree records of the *Danish Doggen*, they were all born in Germany. It was not until the 1880s that the official German name for the breed was fully agreed and from that time it has been called the *Deutsche Dogge*. In England the breed was established as the Great Dane and in 1884 the Kennel Club recognized it as a breed in their Stud Book. In the early history of the breed there are many unexplained mysteries and a great deal of conjecture but one thing is certain – we owe a huge debt to those who developed this beautiful dog in the beginning.

Modern history is far more tangible as in many cases we can trace the breeding of our own particular Great Danes through the information contained in their pedigrees. In every phase of history there have been static periods when little was worth reporting and this was so during the early 1900s where Great Danes were concerned. The breed made steady progress briefly interrupted by World War One, but possibly the greatest changes in the breed took place from the 1920s until the present time.

Before closing on the early history of the breed it is useful to highlight certain important dates concerning the development of Great Danes. **1880** was the year in which Germany established the name *Deutsche Dogge* as their official name for the breed. In **1883** the Great Dane Club was formed in Britain and indeed remains one of the leading clubs of today. In **1884** the Kennel Club first provided classes for Great Danes at the Birmingham Show, and accepted them as a recognized breed in their official Stud Book. In the same year King Edward VII (then Prince of Wales) requested that cropping of ears should cease. In **1895** the Kennel Club introduced a regulation forbidding the cropping of ears. **1901** was the deadline for the exhibition of Great Danes with cropped ears (but imported dogs could be entered at dog shows as 'not for competition' and their progency could be registered with the Kennel Club). In **1918** and **1919** Challenge Certificates were not awarded and therefore no dogs could be made into champions.

Many changes have taken place in the Great Dane world since the end of World War Two, with the accent on a large number of enthusiastic small kennels. Between World War One and World War Two, the Great Dane scene was almost totally dominated by two very powerful and influential kennels, the first owned by Mr J.V. Rank with his famous Ouborough Great Danes, the second by Mr Gordon Stewart with the equally famous Send kennels; the latter specialized in obedience training and a very high standard was achieved. Although the Ouborough kennels originally housed Harlequins, after only a few years Mr Rank changed entirely to Fawns and Brindles. The Send kennels did not specialize, but housed all five colours. One fact is certain: both Ouborough and Send spent a great deal of money importing the very finest dogs and bitches from the very best European kennels in order to unite Continental with English blood in an effort to create the finest quality.

These two kennels were extremely powerful and had a marked effect on the history of the modern Great Dane – the Send kennels housed over 300 inmates in the peak years. They formed virtually a self-contained unit, with its own bakery where wholemeal biscuit was produced, a huge meat storage facility, its own quarantine kennels and even a fully equipped hospital. No expense was spared in an effort to improve the quality and welfare of the breed.

The Ouborough kennels produced champion after champion with hardly a break between them. Ruffler, Bellovien and Revive were amongst the very best and their dam, Champion Vivian of Ouborough, deserves a special mention.

At the same time that Ouborough was making an impression on the

Dane world, Send was producing winner after winner from two imported dogs – the Fawn Dutch Grand Champion Urlus Volbloed of Send, and the other, also Fawn, Egon Falkenhurst of Send. Urlus, who was the offspring of a full brother to sister mating, producing Champions Mavis, Midas, Egmund, Falstaff, Ulana and Lancelot of Send and, to the only bitch served outside the Send kennel, Champion Bedina of Blendon; Bedina was the first home bred champion bitch of the Blendon kennel belonging to Miss H.M. Osborn. Quite a remarkable feat when we remember that Champion Urlus spent only two years at stud in England.

As can be seen, very few of the smaller kennels of the day had any chance against the wealth and power of the mighty Ouborough and Send organizations. However, Mrs Hatfield's Sudbury Harlequins was one such kennel which succeeded in producing an imposing line of champions including Zarane, Zarina and Zinona. The Trayshill Danes of Mrs Lee Booker and the Blendon kennels also produced champions including Haakon of Trayshill and the imported Swiss Champion Nicette von Eisenhop of Trayshill which were the ancestors of a large percentage of post World War One winners. Miss Osborn was recognized equally for her Champion Benvolio of Blendon, son of Champion Bedina, who won numerous Best in Show awards at Club shows. A special mention must be made of Champion Baffler of Blendon, the last Great Dane dog to be made a champion before the outbreak of World War Two.

In 1938 Mrs Jewell purchased bitches from the Trayshill kennel which were mated to the Blendon strain, thus forming the successful Ladymeade kennels.

Throughout the war years, many breeders were forced into reducing their numbers drastically; shortage of food and items we now take for granted caused the complete collapse of many small kennels. The giants continued to battle on by producing just one or two litters during those times in order to preserve their lines. Upon the return of peace, they once again started breeding enthusiastically. Fawns and Brindles were, as usual, the most popular, whilst Harlequins were almost non-existent and quality left much to be desired. The famous Sudbury kennel had almost given up after the death of Mrs Hatfield's son who had always handled the dogs in the show ring, and this left just two kennels of Harlequins, Miss Lomas's Wideskies and Mr John Silver's Silvernia.

The Blues and Blacks became almost extinct and full credit for the revival of these colours goes to a breeder who is still active today, Mrs Nellie Ennals of the famous Bringtonhill kennels. She was so successful in resurrecting Blues and Blacks that she produced champions in both colours.

Nellie Ennals in serious
mood.

The war years caused havoc with Harlequin brood bitches and so after
the war they had an almost impossible task to compete against Fawns and
Brindles in the show ring. One notable exception was the Harlequin
belonging to Miss Lomas, Champion Frost of the Wideskies, who became
a big winner.

At the very first post war All Great Danes Championship Show,
organized in 1946 by the Great Dane Club, Gordon Stewart judged,
awarding the first post war Challenge Certificate to Mrs Rowberry's
Champion Juan of Winome who was also Best of Breed, and Mrs Guthrie's
Mondaine of Maspound won the Challenge Certificate for bitches.

It is worth nothing that Champion Juan of Winome was the first post war champion in the breed, while Mrs Clayton's Champion Bon Adventure of Barvae, a Fawn, by Rebellion of Ouborough out of Bridesmaid of Barvae, bred by her owner, was the first post war bitch champion. Other champions sired by Rebellion were Rusa of Ouborough, Mrs Rowberry's Jillida of Winome, Mr W.G. (Bill) Siggers's Rivolet of Ouborough, and a very famous bitch, Mrs Robb's Ryot of Ouborough.

One dog that really stamped his mark on the breed was Mr Rank's Champion Royalism of Ouborough: he sired no less than eleven champions including two international champions.

Another dog which left his mark was the Fawn, Fingards King of Kings of Blendon, imported in 1945 by the Blendon kennel from David Fingard of Toronto. This dog sired five champions – Baffleur, Berynthia of Blendon (litter sisters), Jeep and Jezebel of Winome (litter brother and sister), and Champion Blendon Antoinette of Rydene – in just three litters. The grandson of King of Kings, Champion Bonhomie of Blendon, was the only Dane ever to beat Champion Elch Elder of Ouborough, the Best in Show winner at Crufts in 1953.

In the early 1950s Mr Rank and Mr Stewart passed away, their deaths seemed to herald the change that was beginning to take place in the Dane world, for, since the war years, many new small kennels were growing, each contributing much to the breed. Most of these kennels did not have staff on the scale of the giant Ouborough and Send kennels and certainly nothing like the available capital, but they produced Danes of the highest quality. Although Mrs Ennals of Bringtonhill commenced her interest in Great Danes as far back as 1936, she really came into her own after the war. By using Hyperion of Ladymeade, she produced Bahram of Bringtonhill, a giant Black of top quality. Bahram sired the Blue bitch Banshee of Bringtonhill – the first Blue champion bitch in England since 1912, well over thirty years after Colonel and Mrs Cowan's Champion Ranghild of Rungmook, the previous Blue champion bitch. Champion Banshee was bred to Champion Dawnlight of Ickford (both were grandchildren of Hyperion of Ladymeade) and they produced Champion Blacjack of Bringtonhill, the first Black champion dog since Champion Wotan of Send, bred by Gordon Steward back in the 1930s. Mrs Ennals also bred a champion Fawn dog by Hyperion of Ladymeade: a consistent winner, he was Basra of Bringtonhill.

Turning back to Fawns and Brindles: upon the death of Mr Rank the Ouborough kennel name was transferred to Bill Siggers, his former kennel manager. Since the war the Ouborough kennels have bred and shown more champions, including the legendary Elch Elder. He was shown at

Crufts as a puppy and won the Challenge Certificate. He went on to win two more Challenge Certificates at successive shows, becoming a champion on the day he was one year old. His greatest triumph, which was tempered with sadness, came in 1953 when, owned and handled by Bill Siggers, he was made Supreme Champion and Best of all Breeds in Show at Crufts: an honour never before or since equalled by a Great Dane. The triumph of winning at Crufts is obvious, but the sad fact in this glory can only be appreciated when we realize that it was Mr Rank's life-long ambition to win that particular award with a dog of his own breeding, yet fate had ruled that he was not to live long enough to realize this ambition. This wonderful dog Elch Edler achieved what had seemed impossible; what is more, it is thought that Elch Edler was the last Great Dane bred by Mr Rank.

The Foxbar kennels of Mrs Robb were founded before World War Two, and were situated in Scotland. Mrs Robb took over a Brindle bitch from Mr Rank that was destined to make history – Champion Ryot of Ouborough who won for her new owner twelve Challenge Certificates and was Best of all Breeds at the Edinburgh Championship Show in 1949. She was a wonderful brood bitch who produced Champions Raet, Rindell, and Racketeer of Ouborough, the sire of whom was Champion Royalism of Ouborough.

Another pre war kennel that continued after the end of the war was Blendon. It must be mentioned that Champion Baffler of Blendon was not only the last dog before the war to become a champion, he was also a Brindle, and the very next Brindle champion was his own great great grandson, Champion Bonhomie of Blendon in 1951. Bonhomie went on to win ten Challenge Certificates and was Best in Show at the Great Dane Breeders Association Show in London in 1954, the only specialist show for the breed for which the Kennel Club allocated Challenge Certificates during that year. It was at this show that the great Elch Elder was beaten by the four-year-old Bonhomie.

The Oldmanor kennels of the Rev. and Mrs Olive Davies have a very soft spot in my heart, for as I have said in my introduction, this was where I purchased my own first Great Dane. The Oldmanor kennels were originally founded by Mrs Clara Russell, Olive's mother, before World War Two, and unknown to many of the present day breeders, she bred Harlequins. It was not very long before Oldmanor specialized in Fawns and Brindles and this famous kennel was still producing champions until a few years ago. The Rev. and Mrs Davies are still very active in the Great Dane world, and can be seen judging and stewarding for the breed at championship shows throughout the country.

Olive Davies of Oldmanor fame.

Numerous were the champions from the Oldmanor kennels including Minuet, Minuetmiss, Meleta, Moyalism, Miss Monica, Meletalyon and Moyra. The Oldmanor dogs were amongst the best Fawns and Brindles in the show ring during the post war years, with my own particular favourite being Champion Minuet of Oldmanor. With careful selection of stud dogs, including Champion Tellus of Moonsfield, Champion Festival of Ouborough, Champion Benison of Blendon and Champion Saturn of Nightsgift, the undeniable quality of Great Danes in Britain was maintained by Oldmanor.

Champion Tellus of Moonsfield featured in many of the Oldmanor pedigrees and Moonsfield is the name of Mrs Edna Harrild's famous kennels that were founded in 1940 and were producing fine Great Danes until very recently. Mrs Harrild enjoyed successes that tell their own story, with dogs like the fabulous Champion Telaman a top winning son of Elch Elder who won no less than eighteen Challenge Certificates and eleven Reserve Certificates, in addition to winning the coveted title of Dane of the Year in 1964 and 1966. There were many other champions including Tandye, Tellus, Telton, Telluson, Thisildo, Tapestry, Telera, Terrel, Todhunter, Try Again and Tellagirl.

Captain and Mrs E.J. Hutton, with their Merrowlea kennels – yet another famous name of the day – helped enormously with the quality built up by their Champions Mr Softee, Merry Deal, Miss Fancy Free, Mighty Fine and Miss Freedom, all of whom belong in the history of the breed.

Harlequin breeding had, as I have already said, suffered a great setback during the war years, and had it not been for one devoted breeder of this colour we shall never know what might have happened. She was Mrs Joan Kelly with her famous Leesthorphill kennels at Melton Mowbray – the driving force behind our Harlequins – and in 1956 she steered her beautiful Surtees of Leesthorphill to his title. It is interesting to note that Surtees was the offspring of Champions Cloud and Snow of the Wideskies, both owned by Mrs Kelly. Four years later Champion Sutton of Leesthorphill gained his title and in 1962 came Champions Survey, Seranda and Surcelle of Leesthorphill. It was a tough struggle with Harlequins against the massive competition of Fawns and Brindles and only the indomitable character and tenacity of Mrs Kelly saved this colour in daunting competition. Joan Kelly is no longer with us but I shall always remember her as

Ch. Minuet of Oldmanor.

the perfect competitor.

I should point out that I have appeared to name only the successful kennels and their champions, but there were, and still are, the absolute backbone of any breed, the breeders and exhibitors who just fail to qualify their lovely Danes as champions, for many reasons, sadly in some cases purely financial and with others it is a case of being in the right place at the wrong time, one of the shortcomings of our judging system.

Travelling nearer to the present time we have seen the Walkmyll kennels and Mrs Freda Lewis gaining many successes. For the record, her fine champions included Candy, Lotus, Storm, Montgomery and others, bred by Mrs Lewis and shown against tremendous competition in today's show world.

The giant killers have also been seen in competition for top honours and one such was a bitch owned and bred by Mrs Brenda Price, who now resides in South Africa. Sired by Champion Oldmanor Pioneer of Daneii and out of Aliandra of Ancholme came one of the most beautiful Great Danes I can remember, Champion Laburmax Eurydice who gained her title in 1972. It is indeed sad that this breed record holder for many years never produced offspring, for she was without doubt one of the finest.

The restoration of the Harlequin had been achieved by Mrs Kelly and,

Ch. Walkmyll
Montgomery.

taking up the challenge this colour offered, came the Helmlake kennels, still existing and owned by Mrs Karina Le Mare. The success of her Harlequin breeding was due to the importation of an outstanding sire from the Continent, Helmlake Ben El Eick Von Forellenparadies, who was mated to Helmlake Magic Columbine of Merrowlea, producing what I believe to be the best Harlequin of all time. The impact on ringside spectators was something to behold when this giant Harlequin puppy made his debut. It was not very long before Helmlake Chico gained his title, and I was fortunate enough to have the opportunity of awarding this gorgeous gentle giant the last Challenge Certificate he won before his death. From Chico came Montego, Champion Fancy Fashion and, via Montego, another fabulous Harlequin Champion Implicable. Although we may think of Helmlake as Harlequin this is not strictly true, for back in 1972 Champion Simba of Helmlake received his much deserved title, quickly followed by an outstanding bitch of great quality, Champion Helmlake Mahe; following on in their wake came a Brindle with the pet name of 'Brains' because of his uncanny intelligence as a puppy – this big Brindle dog became Champion Helmlake Praslin. We still have the famous Clausentum kennels belonging to Mrs and Miss Lanning whose outstanding dog of the 1970s was Champion Fergus of Clausentum and a

Ch. Helmlake Chico.

flag bearer for the breed indeed.

The kennels of Di and Carl Johnson, who are among the present very active enthusiasts, bear the name Dicarl. Again, their successes, which are numerous, came with the Fawns and such impressive Danes as Champions The Heavyweight, The Weightlifter, The Pacemaker, The Alliance with Algwynne and Champion The Contender of Dicarl, who, although bred by the Endroma kennels of Peter and Rae Russell, became the property of the Dicarl kennels as a very young puppy. This beautiful dog was skilfully steered to the winning position in the Working Group at Crufts, 1981, after gaining yet another Challenge Certificate and Best of Breed. Another outstanding Dicarl-bred Dane was Champion Dicarl Tendellie who was owned by one of the most promising handlers of the period; his name was Shaun McAlpine and both dog and owner were as one, for both worshipped each other – their relationship was perfection. It was a sad day when their partnership ended so tragically with the death of Shaun in a car accident.

A dog that provided a further injection of quality in recent years was Lincoln's Winstead Von Raesac. Imported by Mr and Mrs B. Edmonds of Sherain Great Danes, he was a potent sire and helped improve the breed in this country enormously.

Carl Johnson handling Dicarl The Alliance With Algwynne.

The late young ambassador Shaun McAlpine with Ch. Dicarl Tendellie.

The modern breed record holder Ch. Daneton Amilia.

The present record holder of Challenge Certificates in the breed is Champion Daneton Amilia, bred by Joy and Ivan Butcher, owned and shown by Mr and Mrs Mike Duckworth. This outstanding bitch has not arrived from one of the big names in kennels but from a small conscientious breeder. With no less than thirty-two Challenge Certificates it will be a long time before we see her like again.

To all of the kennels mentioned and some which are not, we owe the quality of our present Danes. Will there ever be another Black with the quality of Mrs L'E West's Irish and English champion, Kaptain of Kilcroney, a dog as great as anyone could hope for? Also memorable are the Blues of Mrs Eleanor Walshe and her Sarzec kennels that produced such fine Danes as Champion Sarzec Blue Baron and Champion Sarzec Blue Stewart. We have another first class kennel in Mrs Margaret Everton's Impton Great Danes, who, by importing the best from abroad, and with selective breeding, produced top quality Blues and Blacks. In addition, Mrs Everton's kennel housed another outstanding Black, international champion Impton Duralex Bernando, a champion in four countries and a dog that could boast of being the sire of four generations of Blue and Black champions. The imported international and Nordic champion, Airways Wrangler of Impton, a big Brindle male, soon gained

Ch. Airways Wrangler of Impton.

his British title in the hands of Mrs Everton and created great impact as show winner and sire. At Crufts in 1975 he was awarded the dog Challenge Certificate and went on to win Best of Breed, but another twist of fate happened at this event stealing some of the limelight from that very worthy champion. It was the winner of the bitch Challenge Certificate that sent a bubble of excitement among Great Dane enthusiasts because once again an absolute outsider had achieved what many champions had not, to win best Great Dane Bitch at Crufts. This lovely pale Fawn was originally owned by a doctor and his wife, but due to pressure of work and the damage the puppy did to their home, they decided to part with her. The day the doctor's two children were on their journey to deliver the puppy up to the local police station, they called in at the home of Viv and Ron Bishop, keen Dane owners. One of the children addressed Viv Bishop

Ch. Queen of Carpenders of Vironey.

with what must be a classic statement and question rolled into one, 'You've got a Great Dane lady! Will you have this one?' Viv Bishop took the three-month-old puppy, leading it by the piece of string the children were holding, and agreed to give it a home. It was indeed a very happy Viv Bishop when that same puppy, in spite of having a nasty scar on her right hindquarter due to a burn before Viv owned her, won the Junior Bitch class and then the Challenge Certificate, her first. It took two more years before she was awarded her title of champion: Champion Queen of Carpenders of Vironey had travelled a long way since her birth in a farmyard, rescued from an unknown fate by the Bishops and campaigned to her title. She died peacefully in 1983 as one of the family's pets.

Finally, I offer a toast to the kennels of the current era, especially Nellie Ennals who celebrates her fiftieth year breeding Great Danes and is still as enthusiastic as ever. All of these kennels are striving to keep the Great Dane as its name implies: 'Great'. It is a heavy responsibility which we have taken upon ourselves to preserve this truly wonderful breed.

2 Character of the Great Dane

Your Great Dane is exactly as you want him to be or, to be more precise, exactly as you train him to be, but so is every other dog you may say, and you might well be right, so I will try to explain the difference between a Great Dane and every other trained dog.

When I started to investigate the possibilities of obtaining my first Great Dane, one of the essential qualities was character. I did not want a dog who needed a five-mile walk every day, neither did I desire a dog as boisterous as the fun-loving Boxer. Any breed that was notorious for being snappy was out of the question and so too was the constant yapper. A short-coated breed was necessary because of my idleness: constant grooming is desirable in the case of a long-coated breed. Most important of all, I had always wanted a Great Dane. I once talked to a well-known breeder of German Shepherds (Alsatians) who are highly intelligent creatures; additionally this breeder had always owned a Great Dane – in fact one was his constant companion. When I asked this breeder what he thought the biggest single difference between the Great Dane and the German Shepherd characters were, he swiftly told me that if anyone should tread on the toe of the average Great Dane the Dane would move out of the way and give the impression of being embarrassed for being there in the first place, but if you stepped on the toe of one of his German Shepherds the dog would never forget it and would probably wait for an opportunity to give you a quick nip. The difference is the total lack of malice in the Great Dane. Another side to his character is his absolute need for human company. He is never happier than when he is with his master; be it in the car or by the fireside, a Dane makes you feel very wanted indeed. As a breed they can adapt to all kinds of environment apart from being chained in some yard or other. They are essentially part of the family and when reared with children from being a puppy, they are most trustworthy; even so, no dog should be allowed the total responsibility of being unsupervised with young children who are likely to tease him and fail to understand the old saying 'Let sleeping dogs lie'.

A Dane can be very rough if allowed to be, which is wrong; he can also be aggressive if allowed, which is unforgiveable. The true Great Dane character should be charitable, trustworthy and dignified.

If you require a guard dog then his sheer size and voice is all that is needed to warn off intruders. The use of his teeth is seldom necessary, nor should it be, as he could inflict terrible injuries. So his guarding ability should be confined to his size being the deterrent.

Contradicting my last statement, I am reminded of an incident that happened many years ago when Sheba was, as usual, accompanying me around the Birmingham area. I was driving and she was asleep on the back seat of the car. Whilst attending to company business, I was told by a shopkeeper that a small crowd had gathered round my nearby car. I immediately ran to the car, which was surrounded by a crowd of a dozen or

Honest, I did not dig that hole!

so pedestrians, to find a youth whose arm was well and truly jammed into the mouth of dear Sheba. The police were called and the youth was taken into custody. It was my habit of leaving the car window down for Sheba's benefit (she had to have fresh air) which had caused the real problem. The youth, upon seeing the inviting open car window and ignition keys, decided to help himself. Unfortunately he did not realize that Sheba was lying on the back seat, until her alligator-like jaws took him firmly by his elbow and held on until I arrived. The more he pulled the tighter she gripped but not once did she puncture his skin, only his pride.

On another occasion, I was accompanied by a colleague. We were in a factory canteen attempting to sell frozen peas, when we realized a brochure had been left in the car. My colleague volunteered to fetch the brochure, yet after five minutes had elapsed he returned with a smile and a red face, but no brochure. He then told of his experience with Sheba. Upon his return to my car, Sheba had climbed on to the driving seat. My colleague had attempted to reach past her in order to retrieve the brochure from the top of the dashboard but was immediately leaned on by the resident Great Dane. Not to be put off by this, my colleague tried to sit on the edge of the driving seat which was occupied by Sheba: he would then have been able to reach the brochure. Sheba thought differently and the more he pushed and told her to move, the harder she pushed against him until he eventually sat on the ground. Not once did she growl or show aggression, but even though she knew my colleague had travelled in the car with me all that morning, she refused to allow him entry until I returned.

The predictability of the Great Dane is probably his greatest charm, for as you live with one the more you will know just how reliable he is. You will know if he can be trusted with children or not. You will know his mind as though it were your own, and if you don't then there is a flaw in the bond between you.

Another characteristic that will become obvious to you as you live with a Dane is the absolute hatred he has of being shouted at. I have witnessed the boldest of Danes panic when their masters raise their voices at them. Strangers do not count, but to shout at your own Dane reduces him to a wreck. I feel it is due to his resolute desire to please you at all times, and when you shout at him, it is as though his whole world has collapsed about him until you have lowered your voice, and hidden your anger towards him or indeed others.

To sum up his character I can say with certainty that a Great Dane will be all you would ever want in a dog. I have owned many different breeds, all of them nice in their own particular way, but I have never been without a Great Dane and, hopefully, never will be.

3 Choosing Your Puppy

When you have decided to buy a puppy there are certain well laid out guide lines you should always follow if you are to avoid the many upsets that can take place.

Where do we obtain a puppy? A silly question, the experienced may think, but to the first-time owner it can present quite a puzzle and, if you are not careful, the very first pitfall. Forget the local paper: the chances are there will not be any Great Danes advertised. Ask your local newsagent to obtain a copy of *Our Dogs* or *Dog World* in which you will find a wealth of information and which will include advertisements of breeders with puppies for sale, a column dealing briefly with Great Dane news, plus a number of advertisements showing when and where there are to be general Championship and Open shows. You may wish to visit some shows in order to see a number of Danes together, remembering that Championship shows will be the place where you will be able to see many examples of the breed. It is also at these shows that you will meet many breeders and much free advice can be obtained.

Other places where you can locate a list of breeders, other than in the pages of the dog papers already mentioned, are certain editions of *Yellow Pages* and in the pet columns of the *Exchange and Mart* magazine under the banner of Dog Breeders Associates. This association attempts to maintain a list of reputable breeders and members are expected to adhere to the laid down conditions that enable them to be placed on the list. The final place to locate a list of breeders is the Kennel Club, who upon telephone request will send you a list of breeders as published in the *Kennel Gazette*.

Assuming you have located a number of breeders with the colour of puppy you wish to obtain, you should now telephone a short-list of these people and arrange when it would be convenient to see the puppies. Never arrive at any kennels unannounced for the better breeders will have a higher opinion of a would-be purchaser if they first speak on the telephone.

During the telephone conversation any caring breeder will probably shock you by asking certain, seemingly impertinent, questions in order to check that you will not be wasting your time by visiting their kennels. Always remember the really caring breeder will choose the prospective owner of a puppy very carefully, just as you should choose carefully where to buy from.

Assuming you have arrived at the breeding kennel and made contact with the breeder, ask if it is possible to meet the sire and dam of the puppies. In a great number of circumstances the sire will be owned by

Maggie with Artè and Polo.

another breeder – this is quite normal, remembering that experienced breeders will not just use their own dogs at stud but will use the best stud dog that they hope will improve their own particular line. Again, caution must be the order of the day: if the breeder appears more anxious to show you the puppies before either showing you the parents or interviewing you, then I suggest you bid that particular breeder a swift goodbye. It is essential that the breeder carries out what appears to be an interrogation before allowing you to see any puppies, and you should also appreciate that you may be refused a puppy should the breeder feel the home you are offering would not be correct for a Great Dane. If you are refused, you should retire gracefully and ask yourself the question 'Was the breeder right?'

Presuming you pass the interview with flying colours and meet one or both parents of the puppy you may be about to purchase, *stop* and ask yourself the following questions: 'Were the parents pleased to see me, or did they shy away from me? Did either of the parents appear to be aggressive in any way?' If the answer to the questions is that the parents appeared aggressive or timid, leave the puppies alone, for these tendencies will probably be inherited and the puppies will turn out similar to the parents. If that obstacle is passed and both parents appear very outgoing, the exciting moment is about to arrive – your first meeting with the puppies.

Always remember that, in an all-out effort to prevent the spread of dangerous illness from one kennel to another, it is both good manners and prudent not to visit different kennels on the same day without, at the least, changing your footwear, for puppies are most vulnerable to killer diseases until they have had their full course of preventative vaccinations.

The breeder has invited you into the actual puppy area and you are immediately surprised at the strength and attention these young Danes exhibit, so it is a wise purchaser indeed who visits the kennels wearing something other than their best clothes; ladies should wear trousers, for skirts are ideal for puppies to swing upon and play tug-o'-war games with, and they can ruin tights. Do not attempt to lift a Dane puppy from the ground as they are very heavy and certainly do not enjoy being hoisted off their feet; additionally it is very easy to drop a Dane puppy, causing irreparable damage to those very large but delicate bones and joints. It is important that all of the puppies should be extremely active unless they have just been fed, and that there is no sign of runny eyes or nose in any of them. Be sure there is no sign of coughing or lifelessness, and if you see this then do not buy, for you could be buying problems. You should ensure the puppy you like does not continually run away from you and show signs of extreme shyness: a Great Dane should be bold, and according to most schools of thought it is wise to buy the puppy that comes to you. In plain simple words, let the puppy choose you. When you have finally made your decision, ask the breeder if you can check the puppy's mouth to ensure the top front teeth are over the bottom front teeth in what is known as a scissor bite. If they are not then the breeder should have advised you and possibly reduced the price slightly, for although the average pet owner will not mind such a small fault it is unlikely the puppy will stand any great chance of winning if entered at a dog show.

The puppy's eyes should be as dark as possible. The puppy's feet should turn neither in nor out, which could mean a structural fault or at best indicate a rearing problem. You will probably notice the front knee joint of a puppy appears swollen: there is no need for alarm upon seeing this large knuckle formation, for the growth plates are located in this area and when the puppy reaches adulthood those large knuckles will have all but disappeared. It is worth mentioning that a few veterinary surgeons tend to confuse these swellings with rickets but if there is no apparent pain it is far more likely they are the normal growth plate area enlargements and should be left well alone. The puppy should give the appearance of being a

How did you get so big, Ma?

healthy, happy and probably mischievous youngster and the kennels should be clean, even if chewed, for dirty kennels can mean infested

Maggie with the four-month-old Truly Scrumptious.

puppies and that in itself can be a problem. To finalize this section on choosing a puppy I submit the following verses written by the late Mrs Beryl Lee Booker which emphasize exactly what your puppy should grow into:

If you own a winning Dane,
These points about him please retain.
He must be full of dash and dare
Do anything – go anywhere.
He must be big and sound and strong,
A timid, creepy Dane's all wrong.
Whate'er his colour, he must be
Brilliantly marked, not dingily.
He must not have a perky face
But air of dignity and grace,
His eyes not prominent or light,
But clever, quizzical and bright.
His nose, full, broad and with a ridge,
Most typical above the bridge.
He must not have an ugly lump,
Above his brow like camel's hump,
A lack of stop, or mean 'down face',
And snipy muzzle's a disgrace.

His crested neck he carries high
And holds his head up to the sky.
A dippy back's outside the pale,
And cut-off croup and low-set tail.
Steep shoulders he must then eschew,
Aim for nobility and grace,
A King of Dogs, with regal face,
Who, with his life will you defend
And ever be your faithful friend.

4 The Rearing and Care of the Young Great Dane

The majority of breeders would not entertain the idea of any puppy going to a new home until he is about eight weeks old, by which time he should be fully weaned and used to living away from his mother. By the time a puppy is ready to take up residence in his new home, a great deal of preparation should have taken place including fencing the garden area securely, for we must remember this young Dane will grow quite quickly in both height and strength with the result that an inadequate fence could involve you with neighbour problems, in addition to the dangers of road accidents. All garden hazards must be checked and anything that could be fallen into, or pulled down, has to be secured or guarded. Cold frames can cause much damage to an inquisitive puppy of a Dane's size and weight if they crash through them.

In the house all dangerous objects must be removed. No longer can we afford to leave trailing electric cables from fires, radios and television receivers.

Stairs should be fenced off, ideally with one of those guards used to prevent young children from climbing up. Stairs are especially dangerous to the young puppy as irreparable damage can be caused should he fall. Prevention in all cases is better than cure.

All valuables must be tidied away and so should dangerous toys of the plastic variety. Socks and ladies' tights are another source of danger to the new puppy and many veterinary surgeons will tell you of the heartbreak they have had to face when, too late, they have been called upon to remove unwanted items from an unsuspecting puppy's stomach.

Food should be obtained prior to collecting the puppy (the breeder's diet sheet will tell you what to get); bedding material and a bed should also be at the ready for the new occupant. The actual location of the puppy's night sleeping quarters is of the utmost importance: it must be clean, safe, dry and warm. It must not be an easily damaged area, and should any form of pen be used in the early stages, the boundary should be high enough to prevent the puppy from climbing to the top and falling, causing injury to those big but very delicate bones.

When you eventually collect your new young friend, preparation is once again a must, and a large towel or old blanket should be taken to put the puppy on in the car. Usually the puppy sits on someone's lap during the journey home and the towel will come in handy should he suffer from travel sickness. Remember this young Dane has most probably never been in such a fearsome contraption as a motor car in his short life! The breeder too should be prepared for the collection of the puppy by the new owner and the following items will be made ready by the efficient breeder – Kennel Club documents, pedigree, diet sheet (most important) and a record of worming that has been carried out to date.

When you finally arrive home with your puppy, training commences immediately, not just the training of the puppy but self-training, and the training of the rest of the family, for hard as it may seem, the easiest way in which to settle a new young Dane is by not playing with him. Do not over-fuss him but let the pup find his own way quietly and in his own time.

Sleep, it's more like Piccadilly Circus!

Remember what is normal to you about the home can be an absolute jungle to an immature puppy; every corner and crevice hides danger, every

sudden noise and falling object can put fear into the youngster's heart. We must not allow children to maul the puppy: they should be taught that this is a loving and living creature, not a toy whose eyes are for touching and tail is for pulling. The sooner these rules are adhered to, the quicker the puppy will settle down into his new surroundings.

Training

The untrained Great Dane is an utter menace and a reflection of the owner. Remember, if this puppy is to become the regal creature he should, then training is one of the most important parts of development; as manners maketh man, so too do they make the Great Dane. This beautiful breed has a natural tendency to have eyes only for its owner, but as with other living creatures the final behaviour is only as good as the respect and training it has received.

The first part of the training programme must be feeding and this should take place at the same times every day and in the dog's own dishes, one for food the other for adequate clean water. The puppy should never be pampered. I have often received telephone calls of despair from new owners who say their puppy will not eat and they make the fatal mistake of hand-feeding: this only proves that the puppy is training the owner and not the reverse as it should really be. If the puppy is fit and well the food bowl should be cleared in less than three minutes; if it is not, then take the food away and dispose of it. *Never* attempt to either hand-feed or offer food in a different place. When the puppy learns that he eats or the food is removed, he will be only too keen to clear the contents of the dish within the three minutes. Do not give extra food when the puppy clears the dish with the rapidity of a vacuum cleaner: this is as it should be. A healthy young animal is no different from a child in its enthusiasm for eating and, like the child, its appetite only diminishes when there is illness.

Many breeders have, over the years, suggested that large breeds should be fed from raised platforms for a variety of reasons, including the ease of swallowing and to prevent the front legs and feet from splaying outwards in an effort to reach the ground, causing possible damage. This is of doubtful value for, as I have stated earlier, the maximum time taken for a healthy Dane to complete its meal is no more than three minutes. If the puppy or adult cannot eat from the floor for this period without doing any damage there must be something very wrong with his structure in the first place.

The young puppy must be treated with kind firmness in every respect and throughout his entire life you should resist getting your Dane excited, for this leads to wild racing around and usually ends with something being damaged or someone being hurt, including the dog. Always remember that this young baby is going to mature into a 100 lb-plus adult who will be physically far stronger than you, should he ever need to prove it, and being mown down by a playful 100–150 lb dog, even in fun, is not amusing.

After each meal, the puppy should be taken outside to an allotted place for the purpose of attending to his call of nature. This must always be done immediately after the puppy awakes from the numerous sleeps he has during the day, and I can assure potential owners that it is quite possible to have a young Dane house-trained within three or four days by being vigilant. When taking the puppy out for these calls of nature, a simple command should be used, i.e. 'Do hurry up' or 'Be clean'. When the pup has duly obliged, then and only then, praise should be lavished in an enthusiastic manner; do not let the pup be in any doubt that you are extremely pleased with the performance, and very soon you will be rewarded by a completely house-trained puppy. Just like a young child, a puppy will not be able to control these natural calls throughout the long night, and it is prudent to leave a pad of newspaper near the back door so that the puppy may use this rather than any other place. The golden rule is never to shout at the puppy when you find an accident has taken place during the previous night. You will find that the puppy will be able to go through the night without any mistakes by the time he is about four months of age. As with all training, remember it is far better to lead than to drive.

As the puppy grows you will probably notice a tendency in him to jump up, placing his paws high on your legs or any other available object. This should be stopped, for it may be fun in the beginning but again it is no joke when an adult Dane hits you on the shoulders with full force and dirty feet. The other dangers are of course those nails which can cause great pain and damage should they strike you in the eye or mouth, even if the dog is only being friendly.

Words used in training should be simple, short and crisply delivered, for the dog does not understand long sentences but he will respond to simple commands. The words necessary are NO, SIT, STAY, OUT, DOWN, COME, STAND, and these words must be spoken with authority and no fooling around. After commands have been obeyed then enthusiastic praise must also be given, for we all respond when we know we have pleased our nearest and dearest.

There is a selection of good leather collars available from pet shops but by far the best and most favoured is a chain with a large ring at each end, commonly called a choke chain: quite wrongly, for it is a check chain and its purpose is to offer a loose-fitting but secure collar to which a lead may be attached. When the chain is correctly placed around the dog's neck the lead can be snatched which will close the chain around the dog's neck without causing any damage. When purchasing this type of chain, care should be taken to learn the simple but very important way in which it should fit.

WARNING: Before any puppy is taken for a short walk he must have received a full course of preventative vaccinations against the following dangerous diseases – Distemper, Leptospirosis, Hepatitis and Parvo Virus; so short sessions in lead training should be restricted to the confines of the garden. When you eventually venture out with your puppy, exercise should be restricted in both time and distance, and under no circumstances should a puppy be taken for walks longer than half a mile until he is six months old. All free exercise should again be restricted to the garden or a safely fenced area where the puppy will rest when instinct tells him to. It is very easy to cause permanent damage to a puppy by over-exercising him on a lead.

I cannot stress too often or in too strong a manner that Great Dane puppies should never be played with in rough and tumble games. At all times the giant breeds should be handled in a quiet way if they are not to cause you problems. Keeping a very young puppy under quiet control is relatively easy but as your young puppy grows in size, so will his mind become more inquisitive and the early training should start to reap benefits. But beware, for in many instances around the age of nine months up to two years, depending upon the individual Dane, his brain, like a child's, will show a change of attitude and he will probably cease being the very well behaved youngster you have known so far and will be entering the 'hooligan' stage. Your very immature Dane will decide it is no longer necessary to obey your commands and, to put it quite bluntly, he will appear to have a brain that has turned to water. This is the time of his youth when his master does not matter too much; those of you with teenage children will recognize the signs and just like teenagers this overgrown youngster will seldom respond to bullying tactics, and, frustrating as it may be, we have to adopt tactics so cunning that they are alien to our normal practice. For instance, if you have let your Dane off the lead, in order that he may enjoy free exercise in a safe area, the first sign of this 'new' mood may be his refusal to come to you when called, and – what is more annoying – he may even approach you to within a few metres then without warning commence running around you, probably barking, and doing his level best to make you look a fool. Normally you would be excused for losing your temper, but in this case it will only serve to make him worse, so you have to adopt cunning practices in order to try and out-think him. Fine, you may say, but how? I suggest that when these bouts of wickedness commence you should have in your pocket a simple bribe, either two or three of his favourite biscuits or a titbit of dried meat. Call your Dane very enthusiastically and in a very friendly tone, showing the 'bribe' in your hand. When he approaches hold the titbit in your hand so he may sniff or even lick this forthcoming prize whilst you secure him with his lead. Then and only then are you to give the titbit and make a great fuss of him; don't worry, this problem will soon pass.

Always try to remember you will be judged by your fellow humans on the way in which your Dane behaves, and training should be a continuous practice: training in obedience, lack of aggression and even toilet habits (remember that a hedgerow is better than an open playing field; the roadside verge is far better than a footpath). Ensure you choose a safe area for free exercising, for not everyone will be impressed by the size and obvious strength your magnificent Dane may have and, strange as it may seem to you, some people will be terrified if your big friendly dog approaches them. Always be aware of young children who may get knocked down and injured, and respect the elderly and the infirm. When out in the countryside beware of farm animals, remembering that a Great Dane can quite easily pick up the scent of sheep, cows, horses, etc., and it is much safer to keep your Dane attached to a lead. I have seen young cattle savaged by an over-boisterous Great Dane even though the dog was normally as gentle as a lamb. Instinct stays with animals for many years and many dogs including Great Danes were originally bred for hunting.

Should any form of accident occur involving animals, cars or people, the financial cost could be frightening, let alone the upset to all involved. I would therefore recommend that an insurance policy is taken out covering all eventualities (including Third Party risks which, although not generally known, is a statutory requirement) for veterinary fees and loss. Several excellent companies offer such cover, Dog Breeders' Insurance of Bournemouth and Pet Plan, to name but two. Details are obtainable from your local veterinary surgeon or the breeder of your puppy.

5 Kennelling

What you should start considering as your Great Dane grows from puppyhood into adulthood are his kennelling requirements. Ideally your Great Dane will be one of those lucky ones that will not need an outside kennel, for his life will be spent living in the house. But what if circumstances are not quite that easy and he has to spend his days outside? I say 'days', for if you own just one dog and he is going to spend day and night in a kennel and run, then you should choose a different breed, for a Great Dane needs you more than you may realize. If you intend keeping your Dane confined to an outside kennel then you should seriously consider obtaining two as they will be company for each other and the problems of day-long boredom will be overcome. A Great Dane should never be left alone for prolonged periods and if the purchase of two Danes is out of the question then a smaller breed should be obtained and reared with him.

Kennels are completely useless unless they have a fenced area attached in order that the occupants may exercise freely and keep their bedding area clean. The ideal size for the kennel is not less than six feet wide and five feet deep. A raised platform or bed area should be installed across the narrower side and should be no less than five feet by three feet. If the bed is going to contain bedding other than a heavy blanket, which must be changed often, then a retaining board must be fitted along the leading edge of the bed. The finest material for the Great Dane whose owner has no financial problems is wood wool, purchased by the bale from timber or packaging merchants. Wood shavings too are excellent, although inclined to be dusty towards the time for changing the bedding. The majority of owners and breeders use straw as the second best material. When purchasing straw it is of the utmost importance that only wheat or oat straw is used. *Never* use barley straw as the stems are far too sharp. Another peril in bedding that should be avoided like the plague is shredded paper – it is dangerous. As caring breeders, we tried shredded paper some time ago for it is clean and absorbs much moisture. Unfortunately a thirteen-week-old Saint Bernard puppy we had bred consumed a quantity of this bedding which expanded in his stomach to the size of a football, causing the puppy to die despite swift veterinary treatment. A few hours after this event a Great Dane was seen to swallow a small amount of the same material but the swift removal of this potential killer prevented a second tragedy.

The materials used in building a kennel are numerous, from timber, concrete blocks and brick, to moulded plastic. Timber is without doubt the cosiest but will probably be chewed and maintenance will be necessary. Concrete blocks make an excellent permanent structure but for the average owner the purchase of a timber garden shed is more than adequate. All kennels should be insulated with plywood or better still a water-resistant chip board. Ideally the kennel floor should be solid, e.g. of concrete or paving slabs. If a stable door is fitted then only the lower half needs to remain open, the closed top door offering some protection from the weather. The exercise area or run should be at the very least six feet

Dizie, Scrummy and Blaster in their kennel run.

Great Aunt Sally with
Teka her pal.

high and be a minimum of six feet wide and twenty feet in length, and if possible the whole should be roofed in a corrugated sheeting material. The sides of the run can be of manufactured heavy gauge weldmesh panels which simply bolt into place, or a heavy gauge chain-link material, galvanized not plastic-coated. The base of the run can be of paving slabs, concrete or even pebbles. If pebbles are used they must be no smaller than three-quarter inch grade and will need to be topped up every year. A solid run floor is by far the most convenient and should be laid with a slight slope falling away from the kennel. Cleaning is very simple using a hose pipe and clean water only: disinfectant is unnecessary and can cause chemical burns to paws if not flushed away completely.

All types of kennels need light and a reasonable temperature which should never fall below 45° Fahrenheit: nor rise above 70° Fahrenheit, a carefully sited minimum/maximum thermometer, the type used by gardeners, should be employed. Even though you must be conscious of correct temperature in the kennel, you must be equally certain there is adequate ventilation without direct draught affecting your dog. Light will obviously enter the kennel by the window which should be protected with a mesh guard inside and outside unless an unbreakable plastic window is fitted. In the run area a raised platform of timber construction should be installed so that your Great Dane may avoid lying constantly on the hard and possibly wet surface of the run. We must remember that constant lying on hard surfaces can cause sores to develop on the dog's elbows, hocks and even his hips, all due to his own weight. A dog gets up and lies down many many times in any twenty-four hour period and if this is done on a hard surface you will not need a great imagination to realize the amount of friction and pressure that can take place on the limbs of our heavy-boned, thin-coated friend, who does not have the cushioning coat of a Samoyed or Pyrenean. The amount of money you care to spend on kennelling your dogs can almost be limitless and the suggestions I have made on this subject are the very minimum standards required for the Great Dane.

When the dogs grow old they need the extra comforts they richly deserve, for have they not served you faithfully during the previous years, through all of your fortunes and possible misfortunes? The older Great Dane is not ideally suited to the outdoor kennel and should be allowed to spend his final years in the comfort of the home near to his loved ones. An old Great Dane asks little in exchange for a warm bed and a little food, and as he increases in years, past the age of about his seventh birthday, you will notice that he is more enthusiastic about sleeping than racing around the fields.

If you are fortunate enough to keep your pal until he reaches eight or nine years of age, he will probably spend the vast majority of time curled up in his own chair, or on his bed.

6 Grooming

One of the routine tasks a caring owner should always carry out for a Great Dane, or indeed any breed, is grooming, and grooming is very easy with the Dane simply because there is no great length of coat that can ever tangle. Even so grooming is not just a matter of keeping tangles away or making your dog look smart: there is a far more serious reason for spending a few minutes each day attending to the natural beauty of your Great Dane's coat. Grooming covers many points which include brushing, pedicure, teeth examination and, most important, ear cleaning.

When brushing your Great Dane you must first select the correct type of equipment starting with a rubber hound glove, which, as its name suggests, is an almost square rubber glove with a thumb hole cut in each side to enable its use by either left- or right-handed owners; the face of the glove is covered with solid rubber pimples or cones. By using this very important and inexpensive piece of equipment in a vigorous stroking action it will be obvious that a variable quantity of dead hair will be removed from time to time. If used on a daily basis this rubber glove will not only remove any dead coat, it will also offer a deep stimulating massage through the coat to the skin encouraging the promotion of healthy coat growth and keeping dirt and dust to a minimum. A steel-haired brush is not recommended for Great Danes as they tend to scratch through the coat and possibly cause skin irritation and infection. To complete the simple grooming we should finish off the job by using either a dry chamois cloth or medium soft brush, which leaves the coat with a lustrous sheen.

The next item on our grooming programme is teeth examination, which should be brief but thorough and carried out on a weekly basis. I do not suggest actual brush cleaning but a large uncooked marrow bone given once a week to your adult dog will help in dental cleansing. Any build-up of tartar and staining as the years pass by should be attended to by the vet, who will clean and scale just as your own dentist does, but with the dog safely under a light anaesthetic, a practice that will only be necessary perhaps once or twice during the dog's lifetime.

Nails should be inspected on a regular weekly basis and again this should take just a few seconds. If your Dane is taken for regular walks which include a period spent on hard footpaths, or if he spends some time in a concrete-based dog run, then the need for nail cutting will be almost non-existent, but if his nails do need a pedicure then a guillotine nail cutter or a German veterinary pattern nail cutter should be purchased. The size and toughness of a Great Dane's nails is such that a cutter with a scissor-type action is totally useless, causing both pain and damage to his nails. Care should be taken when cutting the nails and only the very tip should be removed. Take care never to cut into the 'quick' which can cause pain and bleeding. If by accident you do cause bleeding then apply permanganate of potash which will remedy the situation.

Finally you must check and clean his ears, and much caution should be used during this necessary operation. *Never* poke deep into the inner ear with any instrument (this includes cotton tipped sticks) for your dog's ear is a very delicate organ and should be treated as such. Take a soft tissue and very gently wipe around the inside shell of the ear flap – you will probably see a dark brown greasy stain appear on the tissue. Change the tissue and continue until the stain no longer appears. On a weekly basis it is perfectly safe to use about three or four drops of Otodex in each ear canal, holding the ear flap close to the head for a few seconds afterwards, then allowing the dog to shake his ears briefly before wiping them out. Constant inspection in a weekly routine will ensure his ears are kept free of dirt and possible ear mite infestations.

If you start a regular grooming routine with your puppy from the first days of ownership, he will soon respond and in many cases welcome this 'service' as though it were a form of affection from his owner, which it should be. By regular grooming the need to bath your Great Dane will be reduced to almost nil unless he has rolled in some obnoxious material, and only the Harlequin will need to be bathed occasionally in order to keep his predominantly white coat clean. All bathing should be done with luke-warm water and a brand-named dog shampoo which should be removed by rinsing his coat very thoroughly. Remember that if shampooing is done during the winter months you must keep your Dane warm until he is thoroughly dry, and never leave shampoo in his coat.

FLEA

I have purposely left the unpleasant to the very end of this section, but good grooming covers another necessary purpose if we are to be really caring owners. Good grooming will be our early warning system in the battle against parasites like the flea, for where there are fleas, there is always the danger of worms (see the section on worming, page 66).

Fleas are found on the skin of the dog and can cause the host to itch;

because they live by feeding on the blood of the dog, a heavy infestation can lead to anaemia. If a flea is present you will either identify it by seeing a small reddish brown or black insect that moves quickly through the coat, or by seeing black and white grains similar to salt and pepper; these are flea eggs and flea droppings. They are frequently found around your dog's tail or on the neck and the use of a close-toothed flea comb is ideal for checking. The caring owner should keep in stock an aerosol of insecticide, which again is available from your vet; before using always check *how* it is to be used for in many cases your Dane's eyes must be protected from the mist that is emitted. Always treat your furnishings and his bedding if fleas are found on your dog; better still, burn his bedding.

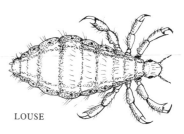

LOUSE

Lice are not very common and usually only affect a dog that is in a very low state of health and kept in squalid conditions. Treatment is the same as for fleas but in all my experience I have never seen lice on any of my own dogs.

Ticks are not very common to the town dweller but they are quite common in the countryside. Female ticks fasten themselves to the dog and the easiest way to deal with the odd one or two is to kill them by applying a spot of methylated spirits, nail polish or any alcohol, then grasp them as near as possible to the head, which will be buried in the dog's skin, and apply a little pulling pressure which will release the tick – there will also be a diminutive male tick nearby. Should you not fully remove the tick do not worry as its remains will very soon shrivel and disappear.

TICK

FINAL CAUTIONARY NOTE on insecticides:
Never use insecticides other than those prescribed or supplied by your vet.
Always read the instructions carefully before using and follow the directions *implicitly*.

7 Breeding

As I have already mentioned, it is my firm belief that you should never attempt to breed Great Danes or indeed any other dog unless you have the proper facilities to do so. Before going one step further let us now consider the fallacies and misconceptions you have probably heard from the 'would-be experts'. A bitch should not be bred from in order to 'do her good' for having puppies will not improve her in looks or condition; on the contrary, even in the hands of experienced breeders serious problems can arise. This fallacy has also been uttered by fools concerning male Great Danes. How often have we heard 'He should be used once in fairness to him'. Oh dear! There must be some exotic food in the world that I have neither heard of nor tasted, so how can I miss it?

One of the problems of using your male Great Dane at stud, even if he is a superb specimen, and I use the term very seriously, is the fact that he *may* become dirty in the house by urinating and marking his territory. He will also be on the look out far more passionately for willing young female Great Danes to oblige him in his new-found pleasure. If you are serious about breeding and you are fortunate enough to have an excellent specimen of the breed who has been judged so by independent and knowledgeable judges, then my comments do not apply, but if he is strictly your pet, your very own pal, then think very carefully and remember cash rewards are never a good enough reason to breed.

The Mating

To the novice there often appears to be a great air of mystery surrounding the actual mating; this in itself is quite amusing, for animals have managed quite well for centuries without the help of man. However, we are now dealing with valuable pedigree dogs and there really is a genuine necessity to supervise any mating that is to be completed, in order to ensure the continued welfare and safety of the two Great Danes involved. It is normal practice for the owner of the bitch to take her to the stud dog, and very rarely the other way round. On the correct day, having made the necessary arrangements with the stud dog owner, we arrive at the home of the stud dog. After a few minutes' introduction, and with dog and bitch owners each holding their Danes on a strong lead, the mating is attempted as follows.

The bitch is held by her lead with the owner taking a standing position at the side of her head, the free hand being used to obtain an extra grip or merely to comfort her. The owner of the stud dog will gently lead the dog behind the bitch whereupon the dog will climb upon the back of the visiting bitch, thus assuming the first stage of the mating position. After a few moments, when the dog has made a satisfactory penetration, he will, being experienced in such matters, remove his front paws from around the bitch and make a complete turn about face. In some cases the stud dog owner will assist the dog by carefully lifting his one hind leg over the back of the bitch. The final mating position is one that mystifies many novices, for when the dog and bitch are 'tied' they will be standing hindquarters to hindquarters facing in totally opposite directions. The final mating position must be held until the bitch releases the dog from the 'tie', and it is at this stage when much damage can be done, for if the bitch or dog are allowed to snatch apart from each other before nature has allowed completion of the act, I can only leave the reader to imagine the consequences. Immediately the mating has been completed your bitch should be returned to your car, where she may rest and wash herself. Many schools of thought prefer the bitch not to urinate for a period of about thirty minutes.

Special vigilance should be taken when the two animals are about to separate from the final mating position, for sometimes at this point there may be a very slight hint of pain causing the bitch to snap at the dog. The bitch may whine, cry or grunt during the actual tie: this is very normal and no owner should become alarmed. Even with this obviously natural act there can be snags, the biggest being when the bitch is not ready or may even have gone past the correct day of mating. If this is so, a forced mating should never be attempted for it can frighten and confuse the female, making further attempts on a different day more difficult than necessary. If the female resents the stud dog or both appear disinterested it is reasonably obvious the bitch is not standing in heat. A slightly nervous bitch, or a bitch that prefers to play, will have to be held but, as I have already said, the bitch should be under complete control throughout the mating and if she shows aggression to the male, a muzzle may have to be applied.

One of the expressions used during matings is a 'tie' and to explain fully to those who are not familiar with the term, the following is what takes place.

The male will penetrate the female by thrusting forward; at full penetration he will start to move his hind legs in a treading motion up and down instead of pushing forward. The bulbus glandis of the penis swells and is gripped by the vulva of the female making the 'tie'. Great Danes will remain tied for anything from five minutes to an hour, with the usual time being around twenty minutes, but should the dogs remain tied for longer than an hour a very careful course of action should be taken. *Do not* throw water over a pair of tied dogs as this practice can result in the most horrific injuries. Instead, return the male to the original first stage of mating position with his front legs around the ribs of the female, then push on his rump whilst the bitch is held very firmly which will increase his depth of penetration. This will relieve any constricting effect of the vaginal ring and the dogs should then slide apart. If after a number of attempts the results remain negative, send for the veterinary surgeon immediately and hold the dogs in position until he arrives. Fortunately this problem is rare.

There are a few points we should consider, points that many experienced breeders unfortunately take for granted. Dogs, like people, are subject to psychological problems, and in the case of the dog that refuses to mate, these psychological problems are far more often the cause and trouble than physical or hormonal problems. It may be that the dog has become shy of mating due to being attacked by a visiting female, and most certainly if an owner continually scolds a dog for making advances towards other dogs, or even people, the dog, fearing he will be punished, will refuse to attempt a mating. Other dogs and bitches who are strictly isolated from other dogs may relate poorly to them, preference being shown to their owner rather than to the stud dog or in-season bitch. The possibility of a hormone imbalance is hardly likely. On the rarest occasions I have seen a bitch panic at the approach of a male and throw herself flat on the ground, displaying a very submissive attitude. The use of tranquillizers may be necessary but my opinion is not to allow the mating of dogs with this kind of temperament. If a bitch continually refuses to be mated then it would be wise to have her checked out for possible vaginal infection or constriction or indeed any other abnormality.

The Stud Dog

Before breeding we must choose a stud dog very carefully. The attitude of 'any dog will do' is completely wrong and if this is the attitude you tend to favour then forget about breeding. It is little use choosing a stud dog that

A good Brindle: Ch. Devarro Direct Descendant.

is almost perfect in every physical way if he has a bad temperament, for this will probably show in the puppies he fathers or, to be technical, 'sires'. It is unwise to choose a stud dog because the owner charges less than someone else who has a much better dog; equally it would be as wrong to choose a top winning champion because the stud charge is very expensive. What is important is compatibility. Will the stud dog offer the qualities you would like to see in the puppies, e.g. darker eyes, heavier bones, outgoing friendly personality, etc.? At all times you should give first consideration to improving what you have and if you reach the point where you think an improvement cannot be achieved it is time to stop breeding.

The perfect Great Dane or indeed any other breed has not yet been bred. If you believe you have learned everything about your chosen breed the only sure fact is that you are a fool, for every choice of mating, every puppy you breed and every dog you own is slightly different from the others, and you are always learning if you are a caring and intelligent owner. Another trap many breeders fall into is thinking that by using a top winning dog they will be presented with top winning offspring, or that they would be able to demand a higher selling price for the puppies. Wrong again. Yet a further trap is the 'pedigree expert' who can advise you which dog to use at stud, without, in some cases, even seeing either dog or bitch. They will offer perfectly sound logical reasons why A should be mated to B, and such a mating should produce C. The most significant word in the last sentence is 'should', for that leaves an escape route the expert can use as an alibi when the end product fails to reach perfection. There really is no mystery: if you observe the human race, some of the most beautiful people have un-lovely parents. Pedigree mating should be used as a guideline, but never as the only criterion, in choosing a partner for your bitch. An old and very sensible saying often quoted by experienced breeders is: 'The dog makes the pedigree, the pedigree does not make the dog'.

When you have reached your decision on which dog you would like to use, contact the stud dog's owner and enquire if you can use him, and request the terms concerning his use. It is important that you learn how much his stud fee will cost – be quite prepared to pay the same sum as the cost of a puppy. The stud dog owner may be prepared to take a puppy in lieu of the stud fee, usually second pick of the whole litter. You must establish if they are willing to allow two visits to the stud dog or only one and it would be sensible to have the agreed terms in writing. The mating of your bitch will take place between the eleventh and fifteenth days of her heat. Many breeders prefer two matings within a three-day period, e.g. the twelfth and fourteenth day, for this is the short period of maximum fertility.

Your Bitch

Your bitch should never be bred from until she has reached at least two years of age, and it is clear that she has no hereditary faults, e.g. entropion, hip dysplasia, mouth faults or temperament problems. She should be in excellent health and a good specimen of the breed: remember that you cannot build on faulty foundations and she is going to be your foundation bitch, on which you will place your hopes of breeding equally good Great Danes.

About every six months your bitch will come into season and will show signs of a bloody discharge from her vulva. This season will last for about three weeks and she should be kept away from any males, other than the selected stud dog, until the full period has elapsed, when she will be able to resume her normal routine. Before she starts her season the bitch must have received all booster vaccinations and completed a course of worming tablets. There are many schools of thought concerning the actual mating preparation. Some breeders place the bitch on a course of antibiotics a few

A promising Brindle bitch:
Bengrafton Fayrechild.

days prior to the actual mating, whilst other breeders instruct their
veterinary surgeon to take a vaginal swab in order to confirm that the bitch
is free from any infection. Some stud dog owners will insist upon the latter
course of action being taken before allowing their dog to be used, in order
to avoid possible transfer of infection.

The expectant mother should be treated as normal during the first five
weeks of pregnancy, when she will need very little extra food. After this
period of time she will need an increase in food up to the time of whelping
(giving birth). The amount of extra food should never be more than 50%
and on no account must the expectant mother be so fat as to become really
lethargic. Dates should be noted carefully – the period from mating until
birth averages sixty-three days (nine weeks), although we should keep a

watchful eye from seven days previous to the expected date of birth. Equally we should never leave the expectant mother for long periods of time for many reasons, which include the need to have her most trusted friend with her, to ensure the whelping has no complications and to help her if complications arise. If she goes past the date of whelping and appears to be in some distress, call your veterinary surgeon immediately. There are complications which can arise and you may be able to take care of them, but if this is your first experience, better be safe than sorry. A course of broad spectrum antibiotics should be given, starting five days prior to the expected birth date and continuing until a few days afterwards. This will cover any problems of infection which may be present.

The bitch should be introduced to her new whelping quarters about one week before the puppies are due and I strongly recommend that a proper whelping box is made ready and placed in the maternity room which will be temperature controlled to not less than 68° and not more than 72° Fahrenheit. If possible a heat lamp should be fixed over the whelping box at such a height that will maintain the recommended temperature. Only a thermometer strategically placed in the whelping box can give you that information accurately. A few days before the mother is to be actually delivered of her new puppies, you should include in her diet a daily amount of calcium lactate, obtainable from your veterinary surgeon – this

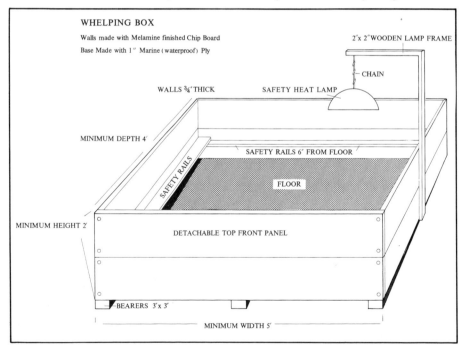

will reduce the possibility of eclampsia (milk fever). The inclusion of added calcium should continue until the bitch has completely finished feeding her puppies. I must repeat that if you have any doubts about the health of the mother at this period, your veterinary surgeon should be contacted for expert advice. It is an absolute necessity that the whelping room is situated where there is ease of entry and exit to the outdoors area to facilitate the brief moments when your bitch will need to relieve herself. The room should also be able to allow for your own temporary occupation, for whelping can last for many hours, so make sure there is a comfortable chair installed.

The floor of the whelping box should be covered with newspapers, and as each birth is complete the papers should be removed and replaced by fresh layers of clean ones. Only when the whelping is definitely finished and mother is well settled with her family should blankets, or the special polyester pile fur fabric rugs used by many, be installed, again remembering that these will need to be changed and washed before re-using, a chore which will seem never-ending as the days go by.

Prior to the birth the mother will probably start nosing and tearing at the whelping box bedding: do not worry as this is normal practice and can go on for a few hours. She will start panting and may appear very restless before and during the 'bearing down' process, which to all intents and purposes resembles straining as though wishing to evacuate her bowels. It will be noticed that a discharge will appear from the vulva. In some cases the dark brown or black appearance could signal a dead puppy, but usually this is not the case. Should no puppies arrive following a discharge of dark colour, then it would be prudent to send for the veterinary surgeon as in extreme cases a caesarean section may be necessary. Upon the arrival of the first puppy you will see it is probably enclosed in what appears to be a polythene-like bag: this is the amniotic sac, and should be removed within thirty seconds to allow the puppy to breathe. If the bitch fails to do this herself, you should tear open the sac and remove it, starting at the mouth and working backwards along the body. Having a soft towel within easy reach, rub the puppy along his back reasonably briskly, holding the head in a downwards position until the puppy starts to utter crying sounds (remember the puppy is very slippery at this stage). Before giving the puppy to the mother make sure the mouth and nostrils are clear of any fluid which might impair breathing.

An alternative and more drastic method of clearing the mouth and nostrils is to hold the puppy downwards, with the head in the lower position and supported by your hand: this is most important in avoiding serious damage to the neck. Holding the puppy in this position, simply ·

swing it in an arc upwards and downwards, stopping abruptly when the head is in the down position. This action should clear the moisture from the mouth and nostrils. When this is done, again, present the puppy to the mother so that she may sniff and lick him prior to cuddling and feeding him.

A further discharge from the mother will follow the birth of the puppy: this is the placenta or after-birth. It does not really matter if the mother chooses to eat this but it is important to count the number of after-births, as any retained can cause serious post-natal infection.

Immediately the puppy is born you will see a cord attached to his abdomen – the umbilical cord which the mother will probably chew through. If she does not chew through this cord, you should take a pair of ready-prepared, sterilized scissors in one hand whilst pinching with the other hand the cord between the puppy and the point you intend to make the cut. It is *most* important that you pinch the cord near to the body of the puppy and make the cut two inches from him, that is to say your pinching fingers will be placed between the puppy and the scissors. Should the cut cord bleed, tie a thin string of cotton around the stump in order to stop the bleeding.

Puppies will be born at intervals varying from fifteen minutes to two to three hours. If your bitch is having strong contractions lasting two hours then call in your vet, for it is possible that there may be a puppy malpresenting. You should also call in your vet if your bitch is unnaturally unsettled or restless for three to four hours even though she may not be having contractions, as this too could indicate something is amiss; it is always better to be safe than sorry.

As the puppies are born and their mother has finished washing them, place them on her nipples in order that feeding can start at the earliest moment: the act of suckling puppies helps the uterus contract. Finally, when the whelping is complete, ask your vet to visit your new family in order to check that the mother has nothing left by way of a retained dead puppy or placenta. He will probably give her an injection of pituitary extract which will aid the clearing out of any uterine debris.

When everything is finally completed and mother and puppies are settled you will notice just how relaxed she has become. This is normal and she should be left in peace for it is important that she should enjoy some well-deserved rest. You can also offer her a small easily digested meal at this stage. There should be no visitors in her room other than you or your vet; she may become over-protective, so accompany the vet into her room. If you have children, they will expect to be allowed in to see the new family, but it should be understood that they must not make any noise or

She had so many children, but Bessie knew what to do.

attempt to interfere with the new puppies or their mother, and the visit should be very brief indeed. Failure to heed these words might upset the mother so badly as to make her aggressive towards the children and/or her puppies. The number of puppies you can expect your Great Dane to have in any one litter could be as few as one or, though it is rare, in excess of sixteen, and if I were to estimate an average I would say eight, but no matter how many puppies there are each one is as precious as the rest, so be thankful when everything goes well.

If there is need for an operation such as a caesarian section then your veterinary surgeon will advise you. Your duty is to watch the expectant mother carefully and if you think she is having birth problems call the vet. He will give the necessary advice and will no doubt reassure you that all will be well as modern drugs and anaesthetics are there to protect the patient, and the success rate of such surgery is very high, provided you seek his help without delay.

IMPORTANT POINTS TO REMEMBER:
Be prepared.
No visitors in the whelping room other than yourself and the veterinary surgeon.
Keep all instruments, including scissors, sterilized by standing them in surgical spirit.
A clinical thermometer is sometimes used as a guide to whelping, and the bitch's temperature may fall from the normal 101.5°F to 99°F or below.

A bumper litter ... Oh dear! I can only count up to ten.

The New-born Puppies

We have already reached the stage where the newly born puppies have settled down with their mother in the whelping box but although we have experienced a very thrilling, if exhausting time, witnessing and helping with the births, our real work has hardly begun.

When the pups are three or four days old you must again call upon the services of your veterinary surgeon for the purpose of removing the dew claws, always from the front legs and sometimes from the hindlegs too. The dew claws are situated in a 'thumb like' position and are of no possible use to the dog. On the contrary, if they are not removed at this stage a far more serious and painful operation, necessitating a general anaesthetic, will be required in order to remove them when the dog is older. If we choose to leave these dew claws intact we must expect them to get accidentally injured or completely torn off in later life. They can get caught in our clothing and, if neglected by incompetent owners, can actually grow round and into the dog's leg, producing a very painful if not infectious condition. So *be warned* and ensure they are competently removed at this early age. The vet will use sterilized scissors to cut off the dew claws plus the claw's bed and he will stop any bleeding by applying either permanganate of potash crystals or, by cauterizing the tiny wounds with a heated instrument. You are advised to remove the mother during this procedure as the possible crying of the puppies will distress her greatly.

If, during the following few days, any bleeding occurs simply apply a few crystals of permanganate of potash to the wound. During the vet's visit it is wise for you to ask him to check the puppies for anything you may have missed and take this opportunity to ask him any further questions.

If you have chosen to breed with Harlequins, then you have some tough decisions which must be faced shortly after any births take place, for it is with this colour that there are almost certain to be mismarks (see the Glossary) which should be culled (humanely destroyed), and if you are not strong enough to have this unpleasant task carried out, then you should not choose this colour to breed with. Completely white Great Dane puppies can be born blind or deaf, or both, and it is not until they are five or six weeks of age that this can be confirmed; to destroy at such a late age is very wrong and even more heartbreaking. Merles (a completely blue blackground with some black patches or spots) should also be culled as this colour too carries the lethal genes for blindness and deafness. It is not unusual for 50% or more of a litter of Harlequins to have to be destroyed for these reasons and it is the main factor determining the very high cost of properly show-marked Harlequins.

Having moved on from the nastier side of breeding, i.e. dew claw removal and culling, we can now settle down to carry out the endless work involved in cleaning the whelping box and bedding. You will notice the mother will frequently wash the puppies' genital areas, not just, as you may think, to keep them clean, but in order to stimulate both bowel and bladder evacuation; even so, a routine check by you is always wise. Should any of the puppies' anuses appear to be obstructed by dried excreta then bathe the affected part using cotton wool and luke-warm water, simulating the action of the mother's tongue in order to aid defecation.

At two to three weeks of age, depending on the size of the litter and the mother's capabilities, weaning the puppies should start, and without doubt the easiest and best way to do this is by using Beta Puppy Number 2 soaked in warm water. Many breeders wean by hand, feeding with finely ground minced red meat with added supplements, e.g. vitamins, calcium, etc., but by using the former method everything is completely balanced and there can be no possibility of over- or under-supplementation. At the time weaning commences the mother should be removed from the whelping room, allowing the puppies to eat freely without the danger of mum stealing their food. Immediately they have finished, the mother should be allowed to return for the purposes of allowing the pups a natural milk feed top-up and to clean them yet again. When the puppies have reached the age of about six weeks they should no longer be allowed to feed from their mother, which necessitates them being totally separated from her. The whole process of weaning should be of a gradual nature so as not to upset either bitch or puppies.

In addition to all of the work you have taken upon yourself in order to ensure your puppies have the correct start to their lives, there are two *most important* procedures which must be carried out. These are *worming* and *vaccinations*, although the latter will most probably be done after the puppy has left the care of the breeder.

Worming

The most common worms found in the new puppy are roundworm and, on rare occasions, tapeworm.

The following procedure is recommended in order to ensure that this problem is completely overcome before it can create a bigger nuisance, and retard the puppies' development. Ask your vet to supply you with a quantity of worming tablets capable of correctly dosing all of the puppies in the litter. Do not cut corners by treating only a selection of the pups, and make sure that every puppy receives the correct dose. The tablets we use are Coopane but your own vet will advise you on this matter. Do not make the mistake that so many inexperienced breeders make by purchasing worming preparations from a pet shop. I repeat, consult your vet first and he will ensure you receive the correct tablets.

Puppies should be wormed at three weeks, five weeks and seven weeks and from then on every month until they are six months old. The worming should be repeated again at nine months, twelve months and thereafter every six months for the rest of their lives. Always obey the instructions included with worming preparations and there should never be any serious ill effects. Other worms, many of which you will never see and certainly need not worry about, are hookworms, whipworms and thread-worms, and if any of these are suspected, again, the only person to consult is your vet and he will prescribe a special worm-killing preparation that should clear the problem, as the treatment for these worms will need an entirely different drug from the normal one used for roundworms.

Two beautiful four-week-old puppies.

Roundworms (ascarids) live in the intestines and range in length from one to six inches. The eggs are extremely tough by virtue of the hard shell which protects them, and they can exist in the earth for years. Dogs become infested by having contact with the soil containing the eggs which enter through the mouth and hatch in the intestine. The larvae are then carried into the lungs via the bloodstream. Whilst in the lungs they become very active, crawling inside the windpipe, eventually to be swallowed, returning to the intestine where they develop into adults. In the older dog very few larvae return to the intestine, the majority remaining in a dormant state in the tissue. When the bitch approaches the later stages of pregnancy the dormant larvae re-enter the circulation until they reach the unborn puppies via the breast milk. Heavy, unchecked infestation of roundworms can cause death, so it is of major importance that the worming programme is carried out. Any puppies having serious infestation will probably take on a very pot-bellied look, they may vomit, have diarrhoea and lose weight. Worms may be seen in the faeces or in any vomited material and can easily be identified for they look very similar to white earthworms or lengths of spaghetti, and if you look closely you will see they are moving. Wherever puppies or adults have been who have suffered any infestation at all, that area should be meticulously cleaned by removing the worms and excrement, then scrubbing with a strong solution of household bleach, taking great care to hose the bleached area afterwards to avoid burning your dog's feet.

To worm a dog and not thoroughly clean the area to which he has been restricted is simply a waste of time. *Always* wash your hands and any implements used before doing anything else. Excrement should, ideally, be burnt.

The *tapeworm* (cestodes) parasite fastens itself by its head to the wall of the gut using suckers and hooks. The body is made up of segments which contain the eggs. Tapeworms can be less than an inch and can reach several feet in length. If you see what appears to be small rice-like particles in your dog's faeces or around the hair of his anus further investigation should be made. Once again your vet is the person from whom to obtain the necessary tablets or medicine, and in many cases he can prescribe a multi-worming preparation which will completely eradicate these little devils. The tapeworm is a strange fellow for he can present himself via uncooked meats or raw fish, but by far the most common way your Dane becomes his host is via the flea. The dog swallows the flea which is host to the immature tapeworm and carried in the flea's own intestine.

Treat all areas where your dogs have been, in the same manner as you have treated for roundworms, with hot water and bleach. Insecticides obtained from your vet should be sprayed on furnishings and the dog's bedding should be burnt.

Vaccinations

Not so long ago many dogs died with terrible infectious illnesses including distemper, leptospirosis, hepatitis and parvo virus but, thanks to veterinary researchers, there are now many preventative vaccines which can be used in order to help protect our four-legged friend.

When the new puppies are about six weeks old your veterinary surgeon should be contacted in order to learn when the course of preventative vaccinations should commence. It should be fully understood that until any puppy has received the full course of preventative vaccinations, he must be confined to his own kennel run or garden and, under no circumstances, should he have contact with any other dog away from his new home. Our own programme of vaccinations commences during the puppies' twelfth week when a combined distemper, hepatitis, leptospirosis and parvo virus injection is given. This is followed two weeks later with the second and final stage of the course.

It is of the utmost importance that you ask your vet to cover every part of these vaccinations thoroughly for it is practically impossible for me to advise which particular vaccines should be used, or indeed the correct intervals at which they should be used. In very recent years, even months, there have been many alterations and improvements to these vaccines, especially to the ones covering parvo virus. What is important is to ensure that all puppy purchasers know how important these vaccinations really are in protecting their Great Dane. Once the full course of vaccinations has been completed, followed by a further week of isolation, the puppy should be perfectly safe to mix with other healthy-looking dogs.

Finally, a word of caution regarding this subject and one that is very important: ask your vet to carry out the vaccinations at your home or in your car at the veterinary surgery, for there is little sense in taking an un-vaccinated puppy into a surgery waiting room full of potentially sick animals, in order to receive protective coverage.

8 Nutrition

The digestive system of a dog is nothing more than a rather complex food-processing factory, where a wide variety of materials from biscuits to raw meat are converted into 'the dog'. The following short verse will describe exactly what I mean.

> It's a very odd thing
> As odd as can be
>
> That whatever Miss P eats
> Turns into Miss P . . .

An amusing jingle based on scientific fact, for what we eat is what we really are, and that also applies to all living creatures including the Great Dane. Generally a dog's stomach can digest the majority of foods in a most efficient manner and, as with human beings, there are some breeds who differ in what they can eat without causing themselves any problems: it is impossible to imagine the Great Dane being able to cope with the variety of food that a Labrador can, without some problems arising.

Good nutrition is dependent on balanced supplies of fat, carbohydrate, protein, vitamins, minerals and water. Carbohydrates do tend to vary in the digesting stages and these must be converted into sugar in the dog's digestive tract before they are useful to him. Carbohydrates form an important requirement in canine nutrition, producing energy source and blood glucose levels.

A maximum of 65% dry-based carbohydrate is advisable in complete foods in order to gain an adequate balance of protein, vitamins, fat and minerals, although some manufactured dog foods of quality contain lesser amounts. An ideal balance for the day-to-day maintenance of an adult Great Dane would be: protein 24%, carbohydrate 53%, oil 5.5%, ash 6%, fibre 2.5%, calcium 1.5%, and phosphorus 0.8%; based on a 100% wheatmeal with fish, meat, bone, molasses, animal protein, milk, seaweed and vegetable oil.

In the growing puppy, from the age of weaning at about three weeks up to the age of maturity, the most suitable balance, without doubt, is the one offered by B.P. Nutrition, and marketed under the label of Beta Puppy Number 2. This excellent product may be analysed as follows: carbohydrate 39.6%, protein 29%, oil 10%, ash 9%, fibre 3.5%, calcium 1.36% and phosphorus 0.99%. When using this product it is of the utmost importance that *no* other additives are used, as whatever is added will

Did someone mention nutrition?

destroy the perfect balance; water is all that is necessary – any other additions could cause irreparable damage to the puppy's structure. Another vital aspect of correct nutrition is the freshness of all foods and, contrary to certain beliefs, the dog that is forced into scavenging is not a healthier animal.

Studies made by the National Research Council have revealed that minerals are a necessity in the dog's diet and are involved in almost every phase of body activity. They maintain a constant 'environment' in the body, whilst providing the bulk of the skeleton, and they are essential for the correct working of the enzyme systems.

The functions of calcium, vitamin D and phosphorus are related. When vitamin D is present in inadequate quantities and the phosphorus and calcium levels are wrong, a number of serious problems can arise, including deficient bone calcification, stunted growth and rickets. Absence of essential vitamins from a diet, or insufficient quantities, lead to deficiency diseases, but just as dangerous is over-vitaminization which has on a number of occasions been blamed for skeletal problems. Each dog is an individual and individual vitamin deficiencies can produce symptoms such as rickets (lack of vitamin D), or black tongue (lack of niacin), although the latter has probably not been seen for many years. The most important point to remember is that vitamins should be given in small amounts, excess quantities do not improve metabolic reactions, and excessive vitamin D can cause calcification of soft tissues such as the liver, lungs, heart and kidneys.

It is generally thought that vitamin C as an additive to the dog's diet is unnecessary as the dog's own system actually manufactures vitamin C, but it has been proved that in time of stress, such as the early growing period of puppies (up to nine months), vitamin C is either not manufactured in a large enough quantity, or is burnt up too quickly, which can cause great problems within the skeletal structure. Over-feeding of your Great Danes together with a deficiency of vitamin C can be a major contributory factor in bone problems such as hypertrophic osteodystrophy, osteochondrosis, spinal stenosis ('wobbler's syndrome') and hip dysplasia. In the case of hypertrophic osteodystrophy the problem will only occur between the ages of ten weeks to nine months and the effects can be not only extremely painful but fatal. In many cases of recovery there will be a permanent distortion of the limbs.

As interesting as the information on nutrition is, there is really no end to the technicalities concerning the subject and, by virtue of its complexities, to continue in scientific detail would serve no purpose to the average dog owner. What does matter is the question: What shall we feed to our Great

Dane in order to completely cover the necessities for general good health? There is an abundance of dog foods on the market today and, as a matter of interest, pet foods command a far bigger market share in the food shops than baby foods, and in fact more money is spent on pet foods than coffee, tea and cocoa all added together. Dog foods are placed before us in tins or packets, frozen or dehydrated and complete forms, and to add even more to the confusion there are no less than fifty different combinations of tinned meats to choose or confuse. It is with a sigh of relief I am able to say that there are stringent regulations covering quality control of these products, which means that whichever brand we choose, little harm will come to our dogs.

In general the Great Dane is not renowned for its 'cast-iron' stomach, unlike the Labrador who seems capable of devouring practically anything, including kennel doors, without any ill effects. Certain tinned products can result in looseness of bowel motions unless that particular Dane has been fed tinned meat since weaning, and as excellent and convenient as they may be, caution should be the keyword. When tinned foods are fed they should be mixed with a cereal product, wholewheat biscuit meal or a cereal-based mixer. Extra vitamins should be used to the very minimum and only if the foods contain none, again remembering that caution should be the watchword when adding vitamins. The next form of feeding, and one that is rapidly becoming the most popular, is the complete type of food and again there are many to choose from. These complete foods contain all the vitamins that are necessary for maintaining the good health of your dog. They can be fed dry or soaked – check the instructions listed on the bag. Most important of all, when feeding complete foods *always* ensure that fresh water is available.

One of the most popular foods for adult Great Danes is ox tripe. Ox tripe is the stomach of the animal and can be obtained frozen from pet shops or in its natural whole state from your local abattoir. This offal can be fed in its raw state or slightly cooked, although I would recommend the former manner of feeding because an offensive odour is produced when cooking tripe. The animal dietician may suggest feeding tripe in large pieces in order to allow the dog the pleasure of tearing at his food, with a separate biscuit meal later. I recommend that tripe is coarse-minced and mixed with a top quality biscuit meal. When feeding in this manner vitamins may then be added cautiously and never exceeding the manufacturer's recommendations.

One of the most important facts concerning the feeding of Great Danes is the amount of food given at each meal, and it is without hesitation that I stress the importance of feeding on a twice-daily basis. This does not mean we should give twice as much food; what it does mean is that the total weight of food we feed in twenty-four hours should be divided into two meals with a gap of at least eight hours between.

Again, let me stress that all of these feeding guides are based on the adult dog, as the nutritional requirements of a puppy are completely different. The two important facts about feeding are as follows:

Always feed a balanced diet.

Never overfeed.

9 Diseases Affecting the Skeletal System

There is little difference in the way many members of the animal kingdom and humans are made, but nature in her wisdom simply allowed animals with two arms and legs to remain on all fours, whilst we humans at some stage in past centuries decided we would walk only on our two hind legs. Dogs have, on average, 319 individual bones which are connected by ligaments, surrounded by muscles and obviously covered with skin. The dog has bones called the femur, tibia, fibula and pelvis to name but a few, and so too has the human skeleton. The main difference between us and them is the size and shape of each bone, and obviously there are great differences within the dog world because of the terrific variation with each breed of dog.

It is important to note the following points if we are to appreciate the various problems that can affect the skeletal system of the Great Dane, and I must emphasize the word 'can' for thankfully many owners will probably never see such problems.

The connection of bones to ligaments is called articulation, commonly called a joint, and if that joint were made by bone meeting bone the ends would grind away each other's surfaces, so a pad has been designed by nature which protects each bone end from such undesirable wear. That pad or protection layer is called a cartilage. The cartilage is very necessary and although made of a very tough gristle-like material it can be damaged by trauma or joint stresses which are too powerful for it to cope with. If this cartilage becomes damaged it may deteriorate and become detached from its correct position, thus acting as a foreign body and causing problems to the joint areas. The hip and shoulder joints are called ball and socket, and they allow movement forwards and backwards, and circular or from side to side, always allowing the ball to seat firmly in the socket. All of the other limb joints are hinges which allow movement only from front to back whilst retaining a stable anchorage to prevent bones from slipping sideways.

A word we must appreciate the meaning of is 'soundness' which is commonly used by veterinary surgeons, dog judges and breeders. There is no mystery in the word for it simply means the dog is healthy, e.g. if a dog is seen to limp he cannot be called sound, for obviously something is wrong within the structure. If a dog is seen to attack viciously we say he does not have a sound temperament, meaning the temperament is not correct.

Skeletal Problems in Puppies

The Great Dane puppy, like any other young animal or child, is most susceptible to serious injuries to his joints and bones caused by incorrect feeding, accidents and careless management. He should never be allowed to gain too much weight, climb stairs or walk on highly polished and slippery surfaces. Under no circumstances should he be taken for long forced walks until at least six months of age. Nor should he be allowed to jump or play roughly with older and bigger dogs. If ever you have to lift a large puppy *never* pick him up by his front legs. Place one arm around his chest and the other around his back legs holding him tightly against your own chest, forming a firm platform to eliminate the possibility of dropping him; the puppy too will feel more secure.

Metabolic and Inherited Problems

Metabolic problems in Great Danes are caused by incorrect diet and rearing. Inherited problems are, exactly as the term implies, inherited from father, mother, grandfather or grandmother and any combination of what we commonly call family history. To be technical, inherited disorders have a genetic or hereditary background which might affect all or some of the offspring. No animal with a serious fault should be used for breeding.

Hypertrophic osteodystrophy (H.O.D.) is a problem that my partner and I have spent a number of years investigating. It is a problem that affects many large breed puppies, and has remained something of a mystery until very recently, although there are many veterinary surgeons who have neither seen it nor can immediately recognize this very painful condition. The disease affects the giant breeds from the age of ten weeks until nine months and can appear any time during this period. It resembles scurvy in humans. Scurvy was first recognized in sailors of the old sailing ship days, who were at sea for many weeks, living off a poor diet which excluded fresh fruit and vegetables rich in vitamin C. It was discovered that by adding certain fruits to their rations the problem was quickly conquered. What was not known in those far-off days was that in many fruits, including oranges, lemons and limes, was the missing vitamin C which could prevent and cure scurvy. Dogs, unlike man, manufacture their own vitamin C and it has been speculated that although the vitamin is being synthesized it is not being utilized by some puppies. This problem is compounded by the fact that this vitamin has only a short life in the body, lasting five hours at maximum.

H.O.D. causes many painful problems and at its worst can bring about the total distortion of the long bones; in extreme cases the skull itself is affected. The pain can be so intense that every bone and joint in the puppy's skeleton can be suffering great pain. The legs and joints become swollen, the temperature rises from the normal 101.5°F to 106°F+. The puppy has trouble in standing and will have greater problems in moving, very often screaming in pain. Confirmation of the problem can be obtained by the veterinary surgeon, by simply X-raying the long bones which will show a 'moth eaten' area above the growth plates. It will appear that a coral-type build-up is surrounding the growth plate area.

In all the cases of hypertrophic osteodystrophy we have seen, we have noted that none of the dogs involved was fed on a complete diet, and without exception the exclusive feeding of tripe or other meats mixed with biscuit meal, with or without added vitamins, has been the cause of the problem. For a time we were greatly distressed when a percentage of puppies bred by us suffered this agonizing and sometimes fatal condition. The majority of breeders have encountered this problem but few care to admit to it. A few years ago we stopped feeding our own puppies on any type of meat-based diet until the age of maturity, and from weaning we feed only Beta Number 2 puppy food, the only additive being water. Our puppies are kept slim but not resembling skeletons, they are lively at all times whilst awake, and the problem of H.O.D. has been completely eradicated from our breeding since adopting this regime. Over-feeding, over-vitaminization and overweight damages the young Great Dane, of that there is no doubt. The over-feeding of your puppy does not produce a bigger dog: his eventual size is governed by his genetic make-up.

Nutritional Secondary Hyperparathyroidism (red meat syndrome) is caused by deficiencies of vitamin D and calcium or by an excess of phosphorus. Over the years it has been discovered that the continuous feeding of an all meat diet can cause the problem. Should this condition be encountered, a balanced diet will correct it but calcium should never be given to a large degree.

Osteomalacia (rickets) is caused by a deficiency of vitamin D and can usually be identified by the bowing of legs, enlargement of the joints where ribs meet the cartilages of the sternum, and in many cases the puppy will show pain. The enlargement of the growth plate areas is probably not due to rickets. The condition is quite rare these days but should it occur a visit to your veterinary surgeon will soon correct it.

Osteochondritis dissecans (separation of joint cartilage) comes under the overall name of osteochondrosis. When certain changes occur in the suspect area they lead to inflammation of the joint which is referred to as osteochondritis, and when the flap of a cartilage floats in the joint fluid an inflammatory condition can occur which is known as osteochondritis dissecans. This problem is quite common in the young growing Great Dane, with males being affected more often than females. The condition usually takes place between the age of fourteen weeks and nine months and is usually found in the shoulder joints. Other sites where the condition can occur are the stifles, hocks and elbows, but it is rare indeed for the latter mentioned joints to be affected. The problem does have an air of mystery, like so many other medical problems, and the tendency for the cartilage to become easily damaged is often thought to be of an hereditary nature. The sign of such a condition is usually the puppy limping slightly, and when a puppy is seen to limp, for whatever reason, he should be rested by confining him to his own quarters or dog run. Under no circumstances should the puppy be allowed to exercise by lead walking or playing with other animals, and if the problem continues for more than three days your veterinary surgeon should be asked to make a close examination of the affected area. In certain cases the condition may correct itself by resting but nearly always surgery is necessary to remove the offending piece of cartilage. I am pleased to say that in the majority of operations to correct this condition a perfect recovery is made.

In all cases of suspected injury affecting joints, *no* pain killing drugs should be given because they can encourage the dog to exercise far too freely. Again, we cannot overlook the possibility of incorrect diet, over-nutrition and over-supplementation as being major contributary factors in some dogs' predisposition towards this condition.

Arthritis (degeneration of joints) can affect our dogs just as severely as it does ourselves and in just the same way. The approach of old age is usually the period when the trouble starts and the larger breeds are affected more than the small ones. We must appreciate the amount of stress placed upon the joints of the larger breeds, and it is very important that we keep our older Great Danes on a strict healthy diet, for being overweight only aggravates this painful condition.

With osteoarthritis we can actually feel a grinding sensation when moving the dog's joints, a sensation many of us will have experienced when our own joints are mobilized. A certain amount of swelling can appear around the affected area but not in all cases. Once again your veterinary surgeon will quickly diagnose the problem if it does exist, and he will treat it with phenylbutazone and steroids for a short period although paracetamol or aspirin do offer relief.

There arc other types of arthritis: septic arthritis, caused by an infection getting into the joint, and rheumatoid arthritis; these conditions are very rare indeed and therefore should cause little or no concern.

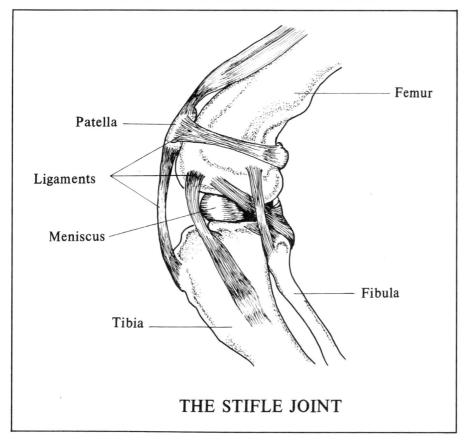

THE STIFLE JOINT

Cruciate ligament damage is explained as follows. Stifle joints are held in a stabilized position by two internal ligaments that are called cruciates. These ligaments cross over the middle of the joint. When a rupture of the cruciates take place pain and lameness occur. This is not a common condition and affects the smaller breeds far more often than the large breeds, but it does happen. Surgery is the only real answer to the problem, which can be caused by trauma, and though the dog will recover well, arthritis and stiffness will set in during the later years.

C.V.I. (cervical vertebrae instability) is called by many names including 'wobbler's syndrome', spinal stenosis and cervical spondylopathy. It is a condition mainly affecting Great Danes and Dobermans. Identification is reasonably simple initially, for affected animals will lose co-ordination, usually in their hind quarters. This will be observed when the dog turns from a straight-line walk, whereupon he almost falls over. He will almost always have some difficulty in rising from a lying-down position: it is as though his rear legs become entangled with each other, and muscle strength does not allow for an easy standing position to be reached. It is thought that the problem has a possible heriditary factor, and the discerning breeder will not breed from stock suffering from the problem. Adult animals are usually affected but there are cases where puppies have suffered. Although it is usually the hind quarters that are affected the real problem is in the cervical spine (neck). There are numerous schools of thought concerning the problem and once again the abuse of certain vitamins and wrong diet have been suspected – too much vitamin D and over zealous use of calcium are thought to contribute.

It is quite possible that in the cases identified in young puppies these could have been brought about following trauma. In the older dog the condition has little chance of improving and surgery will not result in a complete recovery to normal.

Hip dysplasia (H.D.) is first indicated by lameness, and in extreme cases it will be obvious that the dog is in pain. We should never be alarmed at the first sign of lameness but if it persists then your veterinary surgeon should be consulted. As the name suggests the condition occurs in the hip joints when the head of the thigh bone does not sit solidly into the cup of the hip. Although animals whose parents suffered from this condition offer evidence that their offspring will be more susceptible, dogs with no history of H.D. can produce puppies who will suffer the problem. Again over-feeding, wrong diet and too much vitamin supplementation and exercising have been blamed. If the condition has not reached the critical stage an

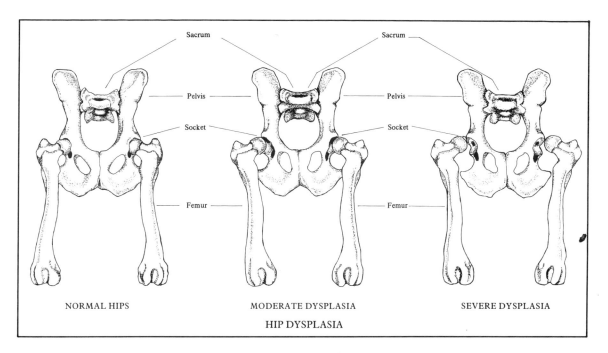

NORMAL HIPS   MODERATE DYSPLASIA   SEVERE DYSPLASIA

HIP DYSPLASIA

immediate reduction of food should be commenced without delay, which will reduce the weight carried by the dog and relieve much of the pressure. From the U.S.A. there have been reports of the work carried out by a Californian veterinary surgeon, Wendell O. Belfield, D.V.M., who claims that high doses of vitamin C can prevent hip dysplasia in susceptible dogs. Although there has been no confirmation via clinical studies, it is hardly likely that a professional veterinarian would risk the wrath of the American Veterinary Association – his research was reported in the Journal of the International Academy of Preventative Medicine.

10 Hints on First Aid

Burns

Burns are caused by heat, chemicals, radiation and electric shocks. In most cases burns will mainly effect the nose, paws and scrotum because these areas are not protected by hair. In certain circumstances the body will be affected by burns from radiation (sun burn), especially in breeds that have their coats stripped during summer time. Where burns do appear on the body it is usual for the hair to fall out upon touching, there might be blisters or ulcers, much redness and the affected areas will be most uncomfortable.

Treatment: Apply cold water or ice packs to small burn areas for up to twenty minutes in order to bring relief from pain. Cut the hair away and ensure the area is clean before applying a topical antibiotic ointment which should be protected from licking by using a gauze dressing. When treating chemical burns apply lots and lots of water and add ointment as above. If your dog has been burnt with acid, dissolve four or five tablespoons of baking soda in a pint of water, mop the area dry and apply ointment as above. *Always use a loose gauze and bandage over the area.*

Frostbite

This nearly always affects the ears, toes and scrotum. You will probably first notice the skin is rather pale in colour, almost white, but when circulation returns the area will start to swell and show much red colouring. The overall appearance will be similar to a burn.

Treatment: Apply soft cloths soaked in warm water, pat the area very gently until dry, then add an antibiotic ointment and bandage the area.

Dehydration

This condition is caused by a number of problems including prolonged illness, diarrhoea and/or vomiting. The simple test for dehydration is by taking a small piece of skin along the dog's back and gently pinching it into a fold: if the dog is not dehydrated the skin will immediately spring back into place; if there is dehydration the skin will stay pinched for some time after being released.

Treatment: Give the affected dog fluids by mouth using a syringe, water and glucose. If the dog is very badly affected your vet should be called in order to ascertain the cause of such dehydration.

Heat-Stroke

A few years ago I was called to help the owner of a Saint Bernard whose dog was over-heated with sunstroke. Although both myself and the vet were on the scene within a few minutes, the poor dog died. You would imagine that this unfortunate creature had been locked in a sun trap without adequate ventilation, but in fact the dog was travelling in a car with the window open. The owner of the dog thought the dog was being cooled by the passage of air through the open window and it was not until the dog had been allowed out of the car for more than ten minutes that he collapsed. I am using this story to illustrate just how dangerous the heat built up in a car can be.

Another cause of heat-stroke can be confining a dog in a concrete area without shade. Always remember the sun moves around, so take great care when providing shade. By far the most common cause is, however, the car; I cannot stress too strongly how rapidly heat is built up in such a death trap.

A dog cannot tolerate heat like a human being can, and in order to keep cool he has to depend on rapid breathing, which in really hot conditions is totally inadequate. Heat-stroke is easily diagnosed by frantic breathing, sometimes with vomiting, thick saliva and occasionally diarrhoea. The dog will very soon start staggering about, then coma and death could follow.

Treatment: Remove the dog to a cool area *immediately*. Immerse him in a bath of cold water, or even a stream or river, provided it is cool. Alternatively hose the dog down using an ordinary garden hose. If he has a temperature of 105°F or over and is near to collapse, give him a cold water enema. A very rapid temperature drop is *vital* if you are to save his life. Sometimes there will be a swelling in his throat: if so, a vet should be called *urgently* in order to administer a cortisone injection for this added complication.

Stings

Bee stings should be removed with tweezers wherever possible and then a paste of crushed baking soda and water should be applied, taking special care not to allow any to enter the eyes.

Wasp stings should be treated with a cold compress of neat vinegar, again avoiding contact with the dog's eyes.

Multiple severe stings to the eyes, mouth and nose should be treated swiftly by a veterinary surgeon who will give antihistamine in order to avoid serious complications.

Pain in the Stomach

This is identified with vomiting, inability to lie comfortably, restlessness, heavy breathing and obvious discomfort. In the case of Great Danes any of these signs should be treated with great urgency as there could well be distension (commonly called 'bloat') – see page 89. You *must* contact your vet immediately you suspect this condition and advise him that you are bringing your dog to his surgery, for if distension is diagnosed then time is of the essence if his life is to be saved.

Dog Bites

When dogs are involved in a fight there are often wounds to dress and they will definitely be contaminated.

Treatment: Clean and apply antibiotic ointment and ensure the wounded party is put on a course of antibiotics or at least treated by your vet with an antibiotic injection.

General Wounds

Cleanliness is the only answer, simply because *all* wounds are contaminated by bacteria.

Treatment: Always ensure your hands and instruments (scissors, tweezers, etc.) are clean before and after use. Cut any hair away from the wound and bathe with gauze soaked in an antiseptic solution diluted with warm water. Following this give a final clean, using clean water only, then apply antibiotic ointment to the affected area. If the wound is large, consult your vet.

Be cautious in your use of antiseptics as by their very nature they can inhibit healing.

Tail Damage

Great Danes very often damage their tails, especially if they have an outgoing nature. You have only to receive a friendly swipe from a passing Great Dane's tail to appreciate exactly how hard the blow can be. Damage to the tail is usually caused by the tail hitting a wall or furniture a number of times, starting with a speck of blood and the tiniest of wounds, but rapidly becoming serious because our demonstrative friend keeps on smashing it against hard objects.

Treatment: Clean thoroughly, as with all wounds, then apply an antibiotic ointment. Dress the wound by wrapping with a gauze and *lightly* bandage. The next tip is vital for we now have to prevent further damage. Obtain a large plastic tube, possibly from your vet: the type used for holding the largest hypodermic syringe is ideal. Place this over the end of the tail, for that is where the damage will occur, and bind it well down the tail with a medical adhesive tape. The use of an Elizabethan collar may be necessary for we must stop the dog chewing and removing the tail protector. Each day the whole dressing must be removed and the wound cleaned and redressed until healing is complete. Unfortunately many Danes have to have a length of tail amputated to conquer the whole problem and if this is the case, do not allow your vet to remove just a few inches, for the trouble will keep recurring. Instruct your vet to amputate the tail leaving no more than about nine inches, which is at least something to wag. If this is done, your happy dog will never damage the remaining short tail.

Anal Glands

Dogs have two anal glands located at about four and eight o'clock in reference to the anal circumference. The openings of the anal sacs are found by gently pulling down on the skin of the lowest part of the anus. If you apply a small amount of pressure immediately below these openings, the anal fluid can be squeezed out.

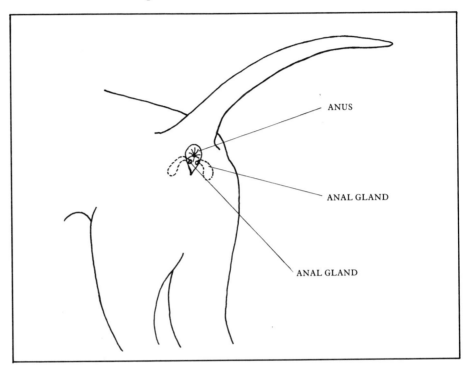

The anal sacs only appear to be of use when marking territory, enabling dogs to identify each other as they do when greeting, by sniffing each other under the tail. Anal sacs are normally emptied when the dog defecates and the contents are liquid and usually brown in colour, but on occasions the liquid may be thick and cream or green/yellow-looking. In all breeds there are animals whose anal glands do not work as efficiently as they should and there are certain signs, e.g. scooting (dragging their bottom along the ground), offensive odour and general discomfort from the rear end, with the affected dog chewing or licking the area.

Treatment: Lift your dog's tail and find the anal sac openings as described earlier in this section. Take the skin surrounding the sac with forefinger and thumb, push in and up and squeeze together. You will notice a pungent odour when the sacs are emptying and it is prudent to use a tissue or damp cloth in order to trap the fluid. It is quite undesirable to have any of the fluid on your clothes or skin because of the obnoxious and tenacious odour.

Warning – should any bloody discharge or purulent-looking material be present, there is probably an infection which should be treated by your vet. In extreme anal problems surgery is sometimes necessary in order to remedy the situation. Your dog's diet should have an extra amount of fibre added: All Bran is ideal.

Pancreatic Enzyme Deficiency

Very occasionally certain dogs of all breeds will suffer from a pancreatic deficiency and there are a number of signs. The greatest sign, when we are quite certain that no worms are present, is the tendency for affected dogs to appear unable to retain any weight and to look generally neglected. In mild cases the signs are a little obscure and there may be diarrhoea and periodic vomiting.

Treatment: Following clinical diagnosis your veterinary surgeon will prescribe a course of pancretin or similar tablets, but if the problem does not clear itself and your vet advises you to keep the dog continually on tablets, the cost can become prohibitive. There is another course of action that can be taken which will be more inconvenient than collecting tablets from the vet, but the saving in money could well make it very worthwhile. Visit the nearest abattoir and ask the manager if he will sell you a quantity of pancreas glands from the slaughtered cattle. By adding between one quarter and one half of a gland to each of the dog's meals the need for tablets will be reduced or even eliminated. The glands will cost only few pence each, far less than any tablets. Try to obtain a bucketful of the glands and individually freeze them for storage in the deep freeze. All that will be necessary is the daily defrosting before use. Note: there are varying degrees of enzyme deficiency but in all cases diarrohea is present.

Diarrhoea

The passing of loose or watery stools is the sign of diarrhoea and in many instances there is overall increased bowel activity. Food in the dog's intestine takes between seven to nine hours to reach the colon by which time the bulk has been absorbed. Over 75% of water is absorbed in the small bowel while the waste is concentrated and stored in the colon, the final product being a well-formed stool. When the movement of food is accelerated it can be for any one or more reasons: it passes through the bowel far too quickly and is evacuated as a liquid, a condition which is caused by hypermotility of the bowel and accounts for the majority of cases of diarrhoea in dogs.

There are a number of reasons for diarrhoea in the dog, including infection, change of diet, change of drinking water source, excitement and scavenging. Dogs can also be allergic to certain foods including milk, eggs, canned food and some complete foods. Remembering that diarrhoea is only a symptom and not a disease, I will list a guide to the types and possible causes:

Consistency

Watery stool – suggests hypermotility with bowel wall irritation (infection)

Foamy stool – suggests a bacterial infection

Greasy stool – suggests a malabsorption problem

Colour

Green or yellowish stool – bowel hypermotility

Black tar-like stool – indicates the upper digestive tract is bleeding

Bloody stool – clots or red blood discharge indicates lower bowel bleeding

Pasty, pale-coloured stool – possible liver disease as the indication is lack of bile

Large grey stale-smelling stool – is an indication of inadequate digestion

Odour

Sour milk or food smell – can be caused by both hypermotility and malabsorption due to over-feeding

Putrid odour – suspect intestinal infection

Frequency

Many evacuations in an hour, small in size and with much straining – suggests inflammation of the large bowel.

Four or five times daily (especially if large) usually means malabsorption.

Treatment: Provided your dog does not appear to be seriously ill, treatment should be as follows. Withold *all* food for twenty-four hours and restrict drinking water to a minimum quantity. If this does not clear the problem then a quantity of Kaobiotic tablets should be obtained from your vet and given to your dog according to the instructions, again remembering not to give any food for a further twenty-four hours. We must also remove any possible source of the cause such as stale food, rubbish bin contents and water. Food and water bowls should be washed thoroughly, with a fresh supply of water made available.

Why starve the dog for twenty-four hours? By starving him we remove the fuel that adds to the problem and so allow the gut to settle, for obviously if there is no food there can be no diarrhoea.

Blocked Bowel

This is the opposite to diarrhoea and very dangerous if veterinary treatment is not sought urgently. The most common cause is the swallowing of an object that the dog cannot pass through his system. The second cause is intersusception which describes a condition where the bowel telescopes in upon itself; or, to illustrate more clearly, imagine a sock that has been pulled inside out. This condition is far more common in puppies than adults. Signs of internal obstruction are vomiting, distension of the stomach and dehydration. When the blockage is low down in the abdomen the vomiting is less frequent; when evacuation takes place it will smell and be dark brown in colour. If vomiting takes place shortly after eating, it means the blockage is high.

Treatment: Do *not* give any purgatives in order to cause bowel evacuation; do *not* give any emetic in order to make the dog vomit; *contact your vet immediately*.

Bloat/Distension

This condition is known by a number of terms including gastric dilation and gastric torsion, but whatever the name it is extremely serious. The reason for this problem, which affects the larger deep-chested breeds, is unknown, although stress has been blamed in certain cases. In other cases over-feeding has been cited and so has sour food, damp food and even stormy weather conditions.

The signs of bloat include restlessness and attempts to vomit, sometimes bringing up a sticky frothy substance. Other signs include the affected dog attempting to defecate and at the same time groaning and whining when pressure is applied to the wall of his stomach. Should your dog develop a condition which you suspect to be bloat take him to your veterinary surgeon *immediately*, for he is in a life-or-death situation.

In an effort to prevent bloat many breeders feed their Great Danes twice daily and, as stated earlier, this does not mean to double the amount of daily food, but simply to divide the normal amount of daily food into two separate meals with at least eight hours between each meal time. Feeding should never take place immediately after vigorous exercise or excitement and no exercise should be allowed for at least two hours after feeding.

Bloat in itself is not the killer and merely refers to a large amount of trapped gas in the stomach. The real problem arises when the stomach twists up to 180°: this is called torsion and can cause not only a most painful condition in the dog, but also death. Even with swift veterinary attention the chance of survival is about one in three and a lot depends on the swift action in seeking that attention.

The interesting facts concerning this condition are as follows:

(a) It affects mainly the large deep-chested breeds.
(b) They may have a history of digestive upsets.
(c) There may be a familial history of bloat.
(d) Bloat nearly always affects dogs of two years of age or more.
(e) Two thirds of bloat cases affect males.

Coughs

Many diseases can cause the dog to cough, including parasites, fungus, bacteria or virus problems. A dog will often cough and sneeze when he inhales smoke or chemicals. The entry of grass seeds into the throat, food particles and even the pulling he may do when wearing a collar can all be causes. Coughs can be caused by a multitude of factors and the following list should be of some help:

1 Spasms of prolonged coughing after vigorous exercise suggest heart problems.
2 A weak gagging cough with much lip licking is mainly caused by tonsillitis and a sore throat.
3 A harsh, high-sounding dry cough is very typical of kennel cough. This cough produces no phlegm.
4 A bubbling moist cough suggests phlegm is present.
5 A wheezy, tight, deep cough is usually related to bronchitis.
6 Coughs accompanied by runny eyes, nose and high temperature point to an infection, possibly distemper.

Coughs that last for a short period of time should be ignored unless they continually return during the following seven days. It is a good idea to keep a bottle of cough mixture in your medicine cupboard, which can help relieve your dog's cough if it persists for more than fifteen minutes. The medicine will not cure the cough but merely bring relief to the affected organs, reducing the frequency and thus helping to eradicate the irritation. If there is no improvement a careful examination will be necessary by your vet who will probably prescribe a broad-spectrum antibiotic. A point that must be mentioned is when and when not to administer cough mixtures. No cough suppressant should be given to dogs who are bringing up phlegm or swallowing phlegm. This type of cough is automatically moving unwanted material from the affected area.

Kennel cough or acute tracheobronchitis is highly contagious to all dogs and if this is diagnosed your dog should be kept isolated from other dogs. Although the condition is not necessarily dangerous to the adult dog it can be fatal in the young puppy and early treatment is a must. Temperature should be taken twice daily and if fever is present it merely confirms there is an added complication. Antibiotics are most important where kennel cough is diagnosed – not to treat the virus, which is unaffected by antibiotic treatment, but to prevent secondary problems. Vaccines are of limited use in the prevention of kennel cough as there are many viruses implicated in the condition. The most useful advice I can offer where kennel cough has been diagnosed is to confine your dog in a warm room, and if a steam vaporizer is available it will help with any problematical breathing. Complete recovery is usual, except in the old dog or sometimes young puppy, but chronic bronchitis can be the aftermath of kennel cough.

How to Induce Vomiting

1 One to two teaspoonfuls of table salt placed at the back of the tongue.
2 Two or three pieces of washing soda, each about the size of a hazelnut, placed at the back of the tongue.

Never induce vomiting to treat the following:
1 If your dog has swallowed cleaning fluid, solvents, alkali or acids.
2 If your dog has swallowed petroleum products.
3 If your dog has swallowed tranquillizers designed to stop vomiting.
4 If your dog has swallowed sharp objects.
5 If more than *one hour* has passed since any poisons were swallowed.
6 If your dog is depressed or in an unconscious state.

11 Know Your Great Dane

Behaviour in the Great Dane is in line with other members of the canine species, for example he has keen hearing, good eyesight and an above-average sense of smell. Within the canine world there are specialist types of dogs who rely more on one set of senses than any other, but the Great Dane uses all of the senses almost equally.

The habits of dogs have always interested me, especially those of young puppies with their mother. One alarming habit can be observed by the novice breeder when the mother is trying to calm down a particularly boisterous puppy. She appears to take the whole of a puppy's head into her

One of the author's breeding.

mouth and then proceeds to open and close her jaws. During this operation the puppy usually becomes quite still and appears to enjoy himself. Many people who know me have seen that I simulate this action regularly with our puppies, taking their cheeks between my front teeth and pinching very gently. The puppy will become quite still, almost as though hypnotized. I must emphasize that I inflict no pain nor even discomfort on the puppy and anyone carrying out this exercise must be very gentle indeed.

It is said that shepherds bite their dogs' ears as a form of punishment to stop them being rough with sheep, but again I must emphasize that the chewing I do to my dogs is very gentle indeed. I am quite sure that inflicting pain is counterproductive in a training situation and inflicting pain at any time is beyond my comprehension.

Playing

I have touched briefly on rough play, which should be out of the question for the Great Dane, for as he grows bigger and stronger the only outcome will be injuries to you, the dog or a third party. Every young dog enjoys playing – it is a part of his natural instinct – and if we research the history

I love you too!

of dogs we will see that playing with litter-mates as a young puppy is a prelude to fighting. Back in history the dog had to fight on many occasions for food and self-protection. On closer observation we will see our growing puppy take a stick or piece of cloth and shake it with much vigour: this again is instinct and the shaking is an attempt to stun or even kill his prey. Always allow some time to play with your Great Dane, but not by wrestling and rolling about the floor, for this will surely make him very rough. Games should be played with a hard rubber ball or ring, but do not play tug-o'-war with him for one day it may just be your coat he starts tugging at.

Behaviour Patterns

There is a definite rank of importance and dominance amongst dogs and we have heard the term 'pack leader' many times. In the wild dogs would often have terrible fights to establish who was the pack leader and the established leader would never be challenged until a new youngster decided he would like to take over the role. Dominance in dogs is very apparent if we watch a group of them together, with much sniffing at each other and stiff upright walking around each other, like two boxers who dance around each other in the ring before one delivers a blow. In dogs the actual fight never needs to start for you will see other patterns emerge when one of the parties concerned starts wagging his tail furiously. This is a signal of *no* aggression or 'I do not wish to fight'; when this happens the dogs concerned will soon begin to play. When we see one dog roll on to his back with his head held right back exposing his throat to the other dog, this is a sign of complete submission and the aggressor will seldom attack. Why should he when his authority is not being challenged? Yet another sign of a dominant dog is the confidence with which he walks past a group of dogs, obviously not the least little bit bothered that he might be in danger. Remember dogs in groups seldom fight seriously, but nervous or aggressive dogs on a lead are in danger of fighting.

Tail Wagging

As we all know, this is normally a sign of friendliness and so too is licking, and you will soon notice that when your own dog starts to lick your hand his tail will almost always wag with pleasure. A dog with feelings of aggression will hold his tail much higher and stiffer than normal.

Marking

A dog, more so than a bitch, will frequently mark out his territory by urinating. It is quite amazing just how many times your own Great Dane will cock his leg at a tree, lamp post or any other vertical object when out for a walk on territory other than his own. A bitch will mark her territory far more often when in season and the reason should be quite obvious: she is leaving a message to any passing canine Casanova who might wish to call upon her.

A strong-headed Blue.

Sense of Smell

A dog is in possession of an incredible sense of smell, far greater than any human being's. This is possibly because the dog has a greater brain area and nasal scent membrane area than we have. To illustrate the difference, liken a man's sense of smell to a postage stamp and a dog's to a large handkerchief. A dog can even memorize the many smells he encounters every day, almost as though he has use of a computer. Not only can he memorize but he can also separate the many smells that he encounters. I have marvelled many times at the miracle our own Danes seem to perform. I will give you an example: when I returned home very late at night with Sheba fast asleep in the car, she never failed to awaken, stand up and give a huge yawn when we were about half a mile from home. Living in an unlit country area she obviously could not recognize anything, yet just the scent of the area was enough to deliver her from her sleep and make herself ready to leave the car.

Be aware of impending danger if your Dane is free from his lead when out in the country, for if he lifts his head in the air, taking pleasure in the scents that you may not even notice, it could be the prelude to chasing sheep, horses or cattle.

Sense of Hearing

Again, the dog makes man look an absolute invalid when we compare hearing abilities. You will observe the comic attitude of your Great Dane when he cocks his head first to one side then to the other when an unrecognizable sound is heard. You will see how still he stands and notice the occasional twitch of his ears in an effort to establish where or what is the cause of the sound he has heard, a sound that you may have been unable to hear, let alone recognize. Again, I will give an example of hearing sense and recognition: when Sheba was alive, she, together with her bosom pal, a Toy Poodle, would be fed at the same time every day. Their time of feeding coincided with the end of the daily radio programme *The Archers*. The programme always opens and closes with the same signature tune. Sheba and the Poodle would never flinch when the tune was played at the start of the programme, but immediately the tune heralded the end of the programme they would leap off their beds and rush to the feeding area.

On the odd occasion when I went out and left Sheba at home, it was amazing how she would ignore all vehicles that came into the street where we lived, except my own car. When she heard my car, long before she could see it, she would rush to the front door barking as though to signal my return.

Sense of Sight

Although a Great Dane uses his eyes as we do there is no doubt that his use of ears and nose is much greater; but there are exceptions, one being the guard dog, another the working sheepdog, both of whom use their eyes almost as much as their ears.

A Binoca Black.

Guard dogs will often sit or lie facing an entrance door or gate in order to watch the area from where they instinctively think the greatest threat may come. The sheepdog will use his eyes in order to watch every single move his flock may make, but at the same time his hearing is on the alert for signals from his handler.

It is often thought that a dog does not have eyesight as good as our own and there is good reason for this belief. If you appear in the company of your dog wearing strange clothes or perhaps a hat that is not usually worn, he may appear surprised even to the extent of barking at the very hat on your head. Never approach your own dog suddenly if he does show these signs; speak to him in order that he may recognize you. Dogs are creatures of habit and the wearing of different clothes, a change of hat or, in the case of ladies, changing from trousers to a skirt, will often cause a dog to be very much on his guard. Dogs are sometimes aggresive toward people who wear uniforms if they are not accustomed to them. Even in spite of what seems poor eyesight a dog will be very aware of any distant object that is moving and my own Danes will often bark like maniacs when they see a hare running across a field some 250 yards away.

It is true that dogs are colour-blind: they actually lack the cones which can identify colours. However, they are capable of seeing differences in depths of colours. To illustrate by example: with my own Danes, more especially Sheba, when my company car was parked at the works' depot amongst at least thirty other cars of the same make and model, she would always run directly to my car which happened to be light blue in colour. Even when I changed the vehicle for a different-coloured model, after just a few days she would pick it out in the car park. She could not possibly have used her sense of smell because, many times, before returning to the car we would circle the car-park in order to let her stretch her legs, returning to the car from an entirely different direction.

One observation is certain: a dog will automatically use each sense as required to the maximum efficiency, be it sight, smell or hearing .

Yawning and Other Gratifications

Most dogs will yawn in a very exaggerated way if they think there is something pleasant about to happen – food, a car ride or walk. As with a human being it is thought the reason for this is to get larger amounts than normal of air into the lungs in readiness for the forthcoming pleasure.

Sometimes a dog will roll on his back in mud, dead birds, rotting vegetation and other unmentionable waste material. He may be seen to rub his nose along the ground with obvious pleasure and certainly after a meal he will often wipe his nose on the soft furniture and your own legs, if you let him. These are all signs of pleasure.

Homing Instincts

The homing instinct of our dogs is quite remarkable and there have been many incidents where dogs have walked over a hundred miles to find their homes. Much more common is the number of dogs whose owners have moved house just a few miles across a small town and their dogs have turned up on the doorstep of the old house. When I lived in Scotland some years ago there was a legendary Bassett Hound who caught the same bus from the village every Monday morning into Stirling and returned on the same bus in the late afternoon. It was generally thought he was visiting his

girlfriend on a local housing estate, and on occasions he was followed by his owners only to give them the slip by disappearing under one of the many close-boarded fences.

They made me carry my own lunch!

Aggression

The normal manner in which a dog shows his aggression is common to the Great Dane too, but owing to the size of the Dane any form of aggression can be very frightening to the onlooker. The expression in a dog's face can be the first sign, coupled with the raising of hair on the back of his neck and down his back and over the hind quarters. Showing the teeth and snarling is a further indication of a very aggressive dog, so beware. Another sign is when two dogs stare at each other in a fixed attitude: this is referred to as 'eyeballing'. Where dogs are gathered in great numbers, such as at a dog show, you must always be on the alert for this and be ready to move your dog away very swiftly, for it is at this stage that either of the dogs will attack and with great speed.

The more you live with your Great Dane, the more you should get to know his habits, his likes and dislikes. I can promise you that one dislike he will certainly have is of people bending over him when he is lying down. This should always be stopped by simply telling those people that he does not like being underneath a bending person, and he is big enough to stroke without this being done.

Never, I repeat, *never* allow anyone to bend over a sleeping dog, as the chances are he will be startled and may snap instinctively, for how can he be expected to understand a tall human being suddenly bending down over him without feeling threatened? Simply respect him and he will both trust and respect you.

12 The Older Great Dane

Dogs vary a great deal in life expectancy and it is unfortunate that a Great Dane will start to deteriorate around six or seven years of age, whereas a small breed like the Toy Poodle will still be young at the same time of life; there is also a difference in ageing between individual Great Danes.

A dog ages in much the same way as humans, with similar signs which are easily recognized. His breath is a little shorter, the stairs are apparently much steeper for him, his hearing becomes a little harder and his eyesight somewhat dimmer. The fire and armchair are more appealing than a 'romp' around the countryside and he should *not* be forced into strenuous exercise. Your male Great Dane should not be used at stud very often and the bitch should not be bred from.

If your old Great Dane has spent a life in kennels now is the time he should be allowed into the house in order to enjoy retirement, and if this is not possible then his kennel *must* be adequately heated and constantly refurnished with clean warm straw, taking care that the kennel is not damp. Remember that old dogs are like old people: they do feel the cold more than their younger kennel neighbours. I say 'neighbours' for it is quite wrong to kennel the old pensioner with a young adult: he deserves to live at his own pace and the presence of a youngster can upset him. *Never* overfeed an old dog – it is cruel and completely thoughtless to allow an old Great Dane to get fat. They need far less fat, minerals and carbohydrates. The old male dog may suffer with diseases such as prostate gland troubles, cancer, heart and kidney disease. Older bitches can suffer with generally similar conditions plus metritis, but not of course prostate trouble. Both can suffer deafness, blindness and paralysis.

It is essential to contact your vet immediately any sign of illness shows itself in the senior Great Dane. When your old pal shows any sign of suffering and the vet advises you that he is in pain you will be faced with the most difficult decision since he came into your life, for he must be painlessly put to sleep, and I can confirm that with modern veterinary medicine this task is absolutely painless. The most difficult part of this sad moment is often the fear of the unknown by the owner. The actual manner in which euthanasia is carried out is by an injected overdose of anaesthetic, and to your eyes there will be no difference: he will simply fall asleep.

My final words on this subject may sound impossible to people of a certain nature, but the owner of any dog should always be with him until the very end. Your presence, as the one he trusts, is a great comfort to him. If you can understand, it is terribly sad for a dog or indeed anyone having to be away from their loved ones at the end of their life, so do try to remain with your old friend even though you may be frightened and upset. Don't be afraid to let your tears fall: your vet will be quite familiar with bereaved owners and will only have words of comfort and not ridicule.

FOR SALE . . . TO GOOD HOME

I was born in the summer,
A few years ago.
Quite why I was born,
I'll never know.

Some folk owned my mother.
They decided to breed.
No reason I know of,
Except for their greed.

I know I was hungry.
I know I was cold.
And they sold me quite early
at just five weeks old.

Owners number one,
Seemed friendly at first.
And life was quite good,
Till my bubble burst.

They started to argue.
Their marriage split up.
And in went the advert:
'For Sale – 4-month pup'.

Some more folk arrived.
The next ones in line.
They treated me kindly,
And life was just fine.

But the Master dropped dead.
And she couldn't cope.
So she sold me again
(I'll soon give up hope).

I now had a new home,
Up in the sky.
We went up in the lift,
Fourteen floors high.

The new folk were kind.
But they left me all day.
I was busting to wee, and
had nowhere to play.

It was boredom I think,
When I chewed up that chair.
They agreed 'I should go
as it just wasn't fair.'

The next home was good,
And I thought, 'This is it.'
They started to show,
And I won – well a bit.

Then somebody told them,
That I had 'no bone'.
And in went the advert:
'For Sale – to good home'.

The next lot were dreadful.
They wanted a guard.
But I didn't know them
although I tried hard.

One night they got burgled.
And I didn't bark.
Tied up in that shed,
Alone in the dark.

For four months I lay,
In that cold, dark shed.
With only an old paper sack
For a bed.

A small dish of water,
All slimy and green.
The state I was in, well,
It had to be seen.

I longed for destruction.
An end to the pain.
But some new people came,
And I went off again.

Well now I'm with Rescue.
And this home is good.
There's walks in the country,
And lots of good food.

There's kisses and cuddles,
To greet me each day.
And I dread the time
They will send me away.

But for now, here I stand.
Skin and Bone, on all fours.
PLEASE – don't let 'Me' happen,
To any of yours.

Joyce Wright, 1986

13 Dog Shows

You are quite sure that you own the most beautiful Great Dane in the whole world and would perhaps like to enter him in a dog show. So you should, but beware, my friends, for the way ahead could leave you with bitter disappointments.

In an earlier chapter I wrote about the temperament of Great Danes, so if you are now considering the possibility of showing your 'Apollo of Dogdom' we must now spend a brief while considering *your* temperament. Few of us can accept defeat as gracefully as we pretend. Human beings are peculiar creatures and dog show people are more peculiar than most. If you don't believe me, then ask any person who has had a passing interest in dog showing. I have witnessed many arguments between people concerning cars, boats, houses, football, etc., but seldom are the emotions as bitter or irrational as they are in the dog show world. It is often said that you can insult many dog owners or their spouses or accuse them of misdeeds, you may even call their children misbehaved and rude, but *never* ever make the mistake of criticizing their dogs. In the eyes of the show dog owner, their dogs are perfect in every way. Even on the rare occasion that they admit to their dog having an 'off day', the majority do not really believe it is their dog, but put it down to the blind stupidity of the judge. My own lighthearted and cynical thoughts in defence of judges in general is that their popularity and 'obvious' knowledge is rejoiced in by the winners, while in the eyes of the losers they suffer from a combination of stupidity, blindness, ignorance and old age.

The only creature who is not upset at losing is the dog.

Dog shows can be both fun and rewarding but, alas, there are very few of us with the same wicked sense of humour that was enjoyed by the late Bill Siggers. He was full of good humour and would kindly tease the unsuspecting at every opportunity. The late Joe Cartledge was another great humorist and although he was not a Great Dane breeder he appreciated the breed very much.

Ch. Timellie Caspian.

The author with his
Challenge Certificate
winners.

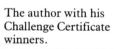

Joe told of a pre-war judge who shall remain nameless. One day he received four lamb chops from a lady exhibitor before he was to judge her breed. At the show the lady in question handled her dog to a second prize. Immediately after the judging had ended she approached the judge and asked if he had received her present, as she could not understand why she had received only a second prize. The judge said that he had in fact received the chops and had found them delicious, but the first prize winner, he said, had sent him a whole leg of lamb. I doubt if the story held any truth but told in this context it serves to illustrate my point.

The exhibition of dogs is extremely popular, and growing in popularity every year. Success comes to those who attend shows on a regular basis, for it is obvious that if you don't attend you will have no chance of winning. Preparation is the key to success and I will take you step by step through the procedure that is required if you are to stand any chance of obtaining a prize card or rosette.

It is helpful if you attend a local ringcraft training class which is usually organized weekly by a local canine society. To find the local organizer or secretary of such a class, contact your vet, the public library or local pet shop, but be sure they do ringcraft training and *not* obedience. There is a

Ch. Aristocrat of Daneton.

technical difference. The ringcraft sessions teach you how to show your dog correctly, they will teach you how to control your dog and get the best out of him in the shortest amount of time. The obedience lessons teach stages of obedience which include teaching your dog to sit immediately you stop walking: this is undesirable in the showring. There are several different types of dog shows starting with Sanction and Exemption shows and ranging to Limited, Open and Championship shows. The first two are really Sunday afternoon fun-type events, a good place for you to practise. The classes are usually well filled with a variety of breeds; Challenge Certificate winners are not allowed to take part. Limited shows are, as the

Taranmur Winstons Belle, a Brindle bitch Champion.

name implies, limited to the organizing society's members only and this type of show is almost always organized by a breed club or canine society. Once again Challenge Certificate winners are ineligible. The next category is the Open show, which as the title suggests is open to all. An Open show will usually have four or five classes for Great Danes; additionally there will be 'any variety' classes. This type of show is normally organized by canine societies, sometimes in association with agricultural or county shows. Breed clubs too will hold Open shows which are confined to Great Danes. Top of the range comes the Championship show and it is at these shows that Challenge Certificates can be won.

In general Championship shows there are a number of rare breeds who are not eligible to win Challenge Certificates, mainly due to the lack of numbers in the particular breeds. In order to gain the title of Champion

Ch. Walkmyll Wonder.

OPPOSITE: Ch. Anset The Smoothie.

Ch. Bullington Corneille,
Olé!

your dog must win three separate Challenge Certificates by three separate judges. The competition is intense and with the average entry of Great Danes in any Championship show exceeding 200, by equally dividing the males from the females you will see the odds are something like a hundred to one against you winning. The shows are divided into classes similar to a handicap system and in order to be considered for the only Challenge Certificate to be awarded in each sex, your dog must win a first prize in one of the classes, then all the class winners compete for the C.C. (Challenge Certificate). After the certificates have been awarded to the best of each sex, the best dog and best bitch are then judged against each other in order to determine the Best of Breed. The winner of the Best of Breed then goes forward to compete in the group to which his breed belongs and in the case of the Great Dane it is the Working group. Should your Dane win the

Working group he then competes for the Best in Show award and in order to have reached this point he or she must have beaten any number of exhibits and certainly several thousand. Best in Show at a general Championship show is very prestigious among doggy people but the Challenge Certificate awarded in the breed classes is the most important to many. Breed clubs also run Championship shows, where Best of Breed is the highest award available.

If you would still like to show your beautiful Great Dane remember my words to new competitors: it does not matter one fig if your dog fails to get a prize, nor does it matter what anyone says about him; what really matters is the fact that you love him and he worships you. Dog shows are just a hobby. The worst dog I ever owned was a big Brindle who rejoiced in the name of Rupert: he was technically wrong from the tip of his nose to the end of his tail, but he was a character – so much so, that I could write a whole chapter on him. I once entered him in a dog show and won a third prize. It was a Great Dane show, the judge was not one of the best and I had only entered Rupert for a wicked bit of fun. So you see, no one ever quite knows what may happen.

Although I have introduced a little humour into this serious subject we should also remember the very important side to the showing of pedigree dogs, far more important than the ballyhoo, the rosettes and even the prize

Look what I have won!

money, although the latter can only be described as token. The single most important point concerning dog shows is that they encourage enthusiastic breeders to continue to breed to the high standard expected. Shows are the only place where any great number of various breeds gather to be seen and compared, and it is obvious that a breed would suffer and eventually hardly resemble the breed we know if such comparison did not take place. In the dog show world the Kennel Club breed standard can be used in a practical manner, for if there was no common gathering place such as dog shows, it is doubtful that enough dogs would ever be gathered together on a regular basis in order to maintain a standard for breeding at all. 'What about those war years?' I can hear you say! In those years when there were no shows, other than the odd local event, we can only be thankful for the tremendous effort and sacrifice made by some breeders who managed to keep a few specimens, some of which were really top quality, in order that we could enjoy the type of Great Dane we now have. Those who were lucky enough to have been born after the Second World War will find it difficult to realize just what the worries of that period amounted to. Dog shows are a real necessity if we are to progress, even though the cynics will continue to suggest they are not quite as honest as they should be. Until someone can come up with an alternative to aid the continued quality of dogs, then we are reliant on the shows.

It is my opinion that every pedigree dog owner should go to at least three Championship shows, to see the real enthusiasm of the exhibitors, to view the different types of Great Danes within the standard and, for a bit of fun, to watch some of the classes and pick out the dogs that they think are best. Remember the judges choose what they believe are the best representatives of the breed, but when all is over it remains just their opinion on the day, and the next show will mean a different judge and probably a completely different result.

Championship shows are almost always benched, which means your dog must be placed on to a platform (bench) and secured with collar and benching chain during the long period he is not in the judging ring.

Open shows are rarely benched these days but you will be expected to keep your dog on a lead and under control at all times. Application to enter shows is by way of a printed schedule, and the details are advertised weekly in the dog press (*Dog World* and *Our Dogs*). Entries for Exemption shows are usually taken on the day of the show.

It is usual that only dogs entered for these shows will be allowed into the show venue and Kennel Club rules are very strict on this subject. If you wish to attend a show without entering your own dog it is better he is left at home, especially during the warmer months.

Ch. Lismear Accolade.

Ch. Helmlake Fancy
Fashion.

Finally, a word on another coveted award called the Junior Warrant. This award can only be gained by accumulating a number of points totalling twenty-five. Only first prize winners from breed classes are eligible, with one point being awarded for a win at an Open show and three points for a win at a Championship show. Wins in more than one class per show count, so two firsts at a Championship show will count as six points. The difficulty in winning a Junior Warrant results from the age restrictions: a puppy cannot be shown until he is six months old and eighteen months is the age limit for this award. A Junior Warrant is so called because at eighteen months of age a show dog can no longer be shown in the junior classes.

14 Great Dane Standards

When we decide to purchase anything, be it a car, house, furniture, clothing or animals, consciously or otherwise we all expect a certain standard, be it of quality, design, service or soundness, but in the majority of cases there must be a forerunner or prototype. There must be at the very least, a design, pattern, blueprint or model, and so it must be in the world of dogs. It is known as the Standard of the Breed. Standards are not developed by all and sundry, for this would mean that many standards would evolve. The results would obviously be catastrophic with each particular breed changing constantly – so constantly, that a true standard would never exist. Obviously if this were to be allowed, we would never have a true standard in height, weight, structure, colour or, most important, temperament.

Ch. Salpetra Silas.

All breed standards in Great Britain are officially issued by the Kennel Club, the ruling body and organization of pedigree dogs in this country. Originally the standards were agreed by the very early breed specialists who formed themselves into breed clubs. Their ideas as to how the standard should be applied included each part of the whole structure of the dog, balance, angulation, soundness, colour and character.

At intervals the Kennel Club approaches the various breed clubs requesting any possible amendments to the standard. It is rare indeed that any recommendations are put forward, other than the possible rewording or clarification of a somewhat vague description. This really proves how right those early breeders and fanciers were in their original specifications for the standard.

There are three main standards for Great Danes throughout the world, the American standard, the German standard and our own which was based originally on the German version. All three standards have a minimum of variation. As I have already stated the standard is the blueprint by which all Great Danes should be judged, and the aim of conscientious breeders is to breed to that standard and not to try to alter the standard to fit their breeding.

Ch. Dorneywood Debonair.

OPPOSITE: Ch. Yaresville Westminster.

The true Great Dane should be a creature of beauty to the onlooker. It should not be a big, heavy, lumbering mass of muscle and bone, even though the size is of some importance. The Great Dane should be regal with an elegance that belies its naturally large build, although elegance should never be confused with lightness of bone, so that the first winds of March look as if they might blow the dog away. The simple picture should be a balance of height, weight, etc.

Ch. Daneagle Alexandra.

Since the end of the Second World War there has been a continuous growth in the population of the breed. In recent years there has been far too great an increase in the Great Dane population, with people who allow their bitches to have litters for financial reward only, and who are all too willing to sell these beautiful animals to anyone when, too late, they realize there is little profit at the end of the day. It is these people who in the main completely ignore breeding to the standard and use any stud dog that happens to be cheap. The only disastrous results from this type of breeding, if unchecked, would be dogs that little resemble the true Great Dane. It is fortunate indeed that a number of breeders adhere strictly to the rules, ignore the 'fast buck' temptations of the ignorant and greedy, and breed to the standard. It is also fortunate that there are dog shows and judges who know and can interpret the standard in its entirety which, combined with conscientious breeding and exhibiting, ensure the standard is maintained.

Let us now go through the British, German and American standards as they are issued by the ruling bodies.

The New British Great Dane Standard

(This Standard is copyrighted by The Kennel Club and is reproduced with their kind permission.)

General Appearance:– Very muscular, strongly though elegantly built, with a look of dash and daring, of being ready to go anywhere and do anything. Head and neck carried high, tail in line with back, or slightly upwards, but never curled over hindquarters. Elegance of outline and grace of form most essential.

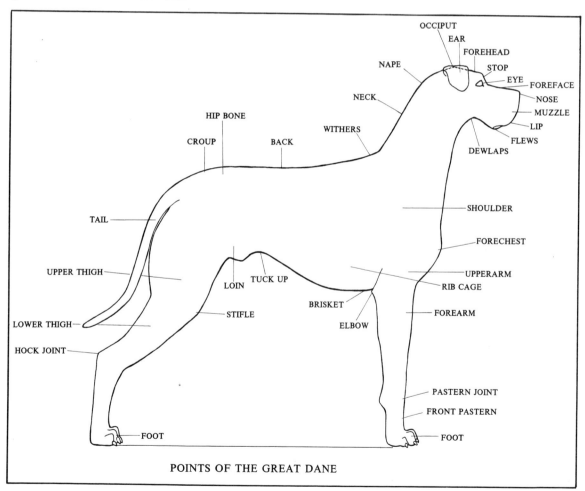

POINTS OF THE GREAT DANE

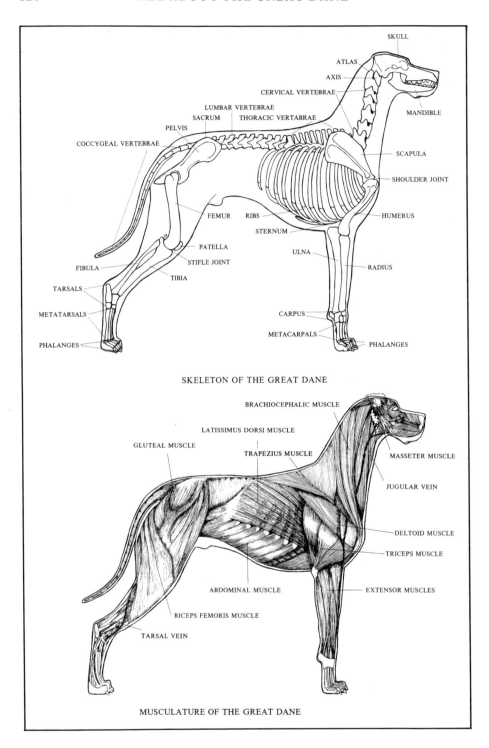

SKELETON OF THE GREAT DANE

MUSCULATURE OF THE GREAT DANE

Characteristics:– Alert expression, powerful, majestic action displaying dignity.

Temperament:– Kindly without nervousness, friendly and outgoing.

Head and skull:– Head, taken altogether, gives idea of great length and strength of jaw. Muzzle or foreface broad, skull proportionately narrow, so that whole head when viewed from above and in front, has appearance of equal breadth throughout. Length of head in proportion to height of dog. Length from nose to point between eyes about equal or preferably of greater length than from this point to back of occiput. Skull flat, slight indentation running up centre, occiputal peak not prominent. Decided rise or brow over the eyes but not abrupt stop between them; face well chiselled, well filled in below eyes with no appearance of being pinched: foreface long, of equal depth throughout. Cheeks showing as little lumpiness as possible, compatible with strength. Underline of head, viewed in profile, runs almost in a straight line from corner of lip to corner of jawbone, allowing for fold of lip, but with no loose skin hanging down. Bridge of nose very wide, with slight ridge where cartilage joins bone. (This is a characteristic of breed.) Nostrils large, wide and open, giving blunt look to nose. Lips hang squarely in front, forming right-angle with upper line of foreface.

CORRECT EYE

HAW EYE

CORRECT NOSE

SPLIT NOSE

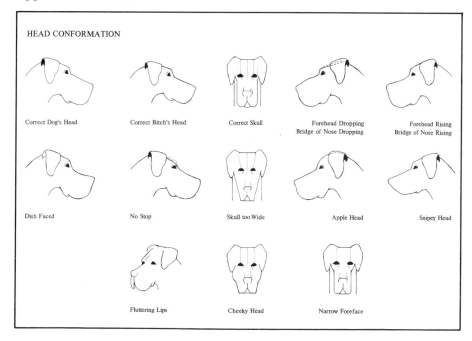

HEAD CONFORMATION

Correct Dog's Head

Correct Bitch's Head

Correct Skull

Forehead Dropping
Bridge of Nose Dropping

Forehead Rising
Bridge of Nose Rising

Dish Faced

No Stop

Skull too Wide

Apple Head

Snipey Head

Fluttering Lips

Cheeky Head

Narrow Foreface

Eyes:– Fairly deep set, not giving the appearance of being round, of medium size and preferably dark. Wall or odd eyes permissible in Harlequins.

Ears:– Triangular, medium size, set high on skull and folded forward, not pendulous.

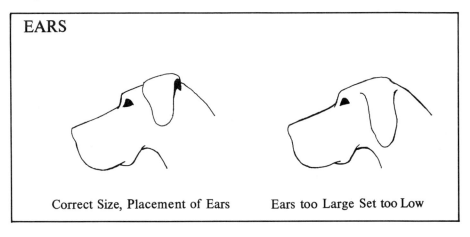

EARS

Correct Size, Placement of Ears   Ears too Large Set too Low

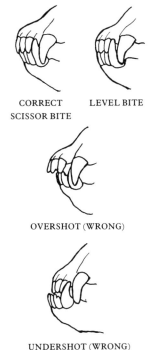

CORRECT   LEVEL BITE
SCISSOR BITE

OVERSHOT (WRONG)

UNDERSHOT (WRONG)

Mouth:– Teeth level. Jaws strong with a perfect, regular and complete scissor bite, i.e. the upper teeth closely overlapping the lower teeth and set square to the jaws.

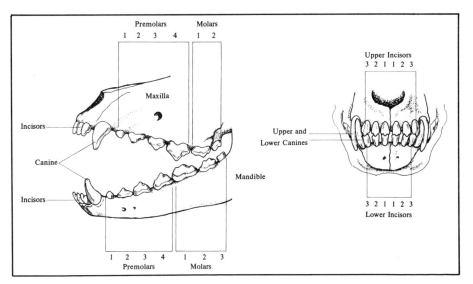

Neck:– Neck long, well-arched, quite clean and free from loose skin, held well up, well set in shoulders, junction of head and neck well defined.

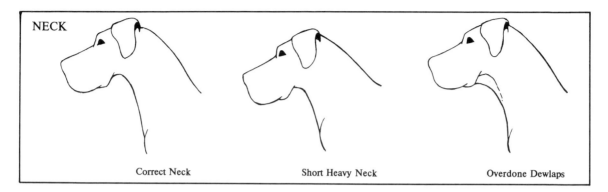

NECK

Correct Neck   Short Heavy Neck   Overdone Dewlaps

Forequarters:– Shoulders muscular, not loaded, well sloped back, with elbows well under body. Forelegs perfectly straight with big flat bone.

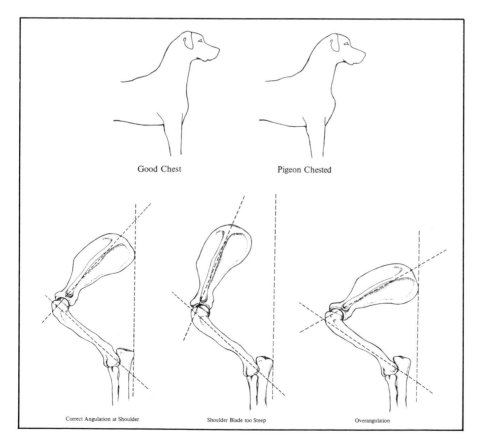

Good Chest   Pigeon Chested

Correct Angulation at Shoulder   Shoulder Blade too Steep   Overangulation

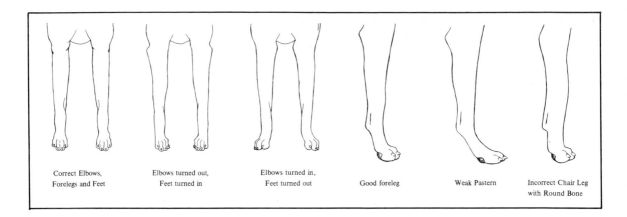

Correct Elbows, Forelegs and Feet

Elbows turned out, Feet turned in

Elbows turned in, Feet turned out

Good foreleg

Weak Pastern

Incorrect Chair Leg with Round Bone

Body:– Very deep, brisket reaching elbow, ribs well sprung, belly well drawn up. Back and loins strong, latter slightly arched.

Rib Cage and Shoulder Blade Structure

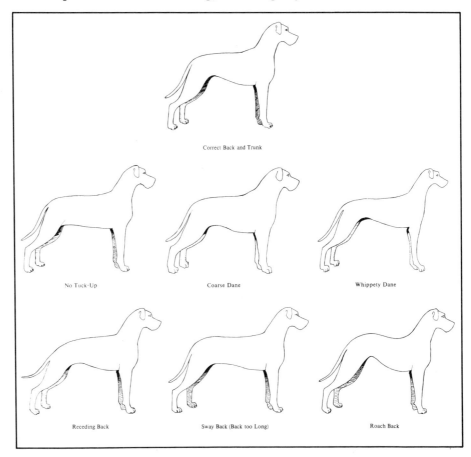

Correct Back and Trunk

No Tuck-Up

Coarse Dane

Whippety Dane

Receding Back

Sway Back (Back too Long)

Roach Back

Hindquarters:– Extremely muscular, giving strength and galloping power. Second thigh long and well developed, good turn of stifle, hocks set low, turning neither in nor out.

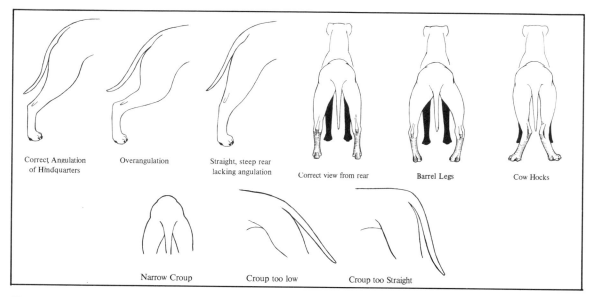

Correct Angulation of Hindquarters

Overangulation

Straight, steep rear lacking angulation

Correct view from rear

Barrel Legs

Cow Hocks

Narrow Croup

Croup too low

Croup too Straight

Feet:– Cat-like, turning neither in nor out. Toes well arched and close, nails strong and curved. Nails preferably dark in all coat colours, except Harlequins, where light are permissible.

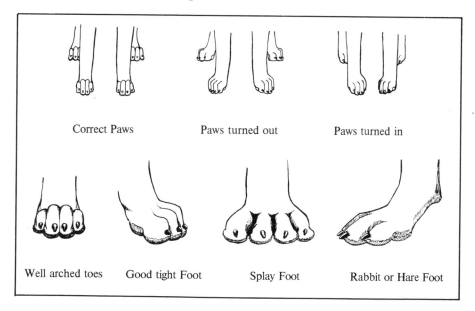

Correct Paws

Paws turned out

Paws turned in

Well arched toes

Good tight Foot

Splay Foot

Rabbit or Hare Foot

Gait/movement:– Action lithe, springy and free, covering ground well. Hocks move freely with driving action, head carried high.

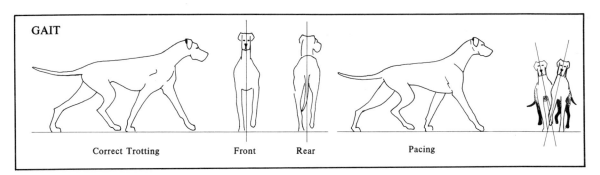

Tail:– Thick at the root, tapering towards end, reaching to or just below hocks. Carried in straight line level with back, when dog is moving, slightly curved towards end, but never curling or carried over back.

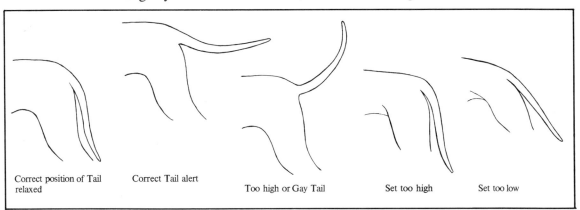

Coat:– Short, dense and sleek looking, never inclined to roughness.

Colour:–

(a) Brindles must be striped, ground colour from lightest buff to deepest orange, stripes always black, eyes and nails preferably dark, dark shadings on head and ears acceptable.

(b) Fawns, colour varies from lightest buff to deepest orange, dark shadings on head and ears acceptable, eyes and nails preferably dark.

(c) Blues, colour varies from light grey to deep slate, the nose and eyes may be blue.

(d) Blacks, black is black. In all above colours white is only permissible on chest and feet, but it is not desirable even there. Nose always black, except in Blues and Harlequins. Eyes and nails preferably dark.

(e) Harlequins, pure white underground with preferably all black patches or all blue patches, having appearance of being torn. Light nails permissible. In Harlequins, wall-eyes, pink noses, or butterfly noses permissible but not desirable.

Weight and size:– Minimum height of an adult dog over eighteen months, 76cm (30ins), bitch 71cm (28ins). Weight, minimum weight over eighteen months: dogs 54kgs (120lbs), bitches 46 kgs (100lbs).

Faults:– Any departure from the foregoing points should be considered a fault and the seriousness with which the fault should be regarded should be in exact proportion to its degree.

Notes:– Male animals should have two apparently normal testicles fully descended into the scrotum.

The German Great Dane Standard

(This Standard is copyrighted by the Deutscher Doggen Club and is reproduced with their kind permission.)

General appearance and character:– The Great Dane combines pride, strength and elegance in its noble appearance and big, strong, well-coupled body. It is the Apollo of all the breeds of dogs. The Dane strikes one by its very expressive head; it does not show any nervousness even in the greatest excitement, and has the appearance of a noble statue. In temperament it is friendly, loving and affectionate with its masters, especially with children, but retiring and mistrustful with strangers. In time of danger the dog is courageous and not afraid of attacks, caring only for the defence of its master and the latter's property.

Head:– Elongated, narrow, striking, full of expression, finely chiselled (especially the part under the eyes), with strongly accentuated stop. Seen from the side, the brow should be sharply broken off from the bridge of the nose. The forehead and bridge of the nose must run into each other in a straight and parallel line. Seen from the front the head must appear narrow, the bridge of the nose must be as broad as possible; the cheek muscles should be only slightly accentuated, but in no case must they be prominent. The muzzle must be full of lip, as much as possible vertically blunted in front, and show well-accentuated lip-angle. The underjaw should be neither protruding nor retrograding. The same length as the back of the head, from the stop to the slightly accentuated occiput. Seen from all sides, the head should appear angular and settled in its outer lines, but at the same time it should harmonize entirely with the general appearance of the Great Dane in every way. **Faults** – Falling-off line of brow; an elevated, falling-off or compressed bridge of nose; too little or no stop; too narrow a bridge of nose; the back of the head wedge-shaped; too round a skull (apple head); cheeks too pronounced; snipy muzzle. Also loose lips hanging over the underjaw, which can be deceptive as to a full, deep muzzle. It is preferable for the head to be short and striking, rather than long, shallow and expressionless.

Eyes (in general):– Of medium size, round, as dark as possible, with gay, hearty expression, the eyebrows well developed. **Faults** – Eyes light, cutting, amber-yellow, light blue or water blue, or of two different colours; too low-hanging eyelids with prominent tear glands or very red conjunctiva tunica.

Ears:– Set on high, not too far apart, of good length, cropped to a point. **Faults** – Ears set too low, laterally, cropped too short or not uniformly; standing too much over or even lying on the head; not carried erect or semi-drooping ears (uncropped Danes should not win).

Nose:– Large, black, running in a straight line with the bridge. **Faults** – Nose light-coloured, with spots or cleft.

Teeth:– Large and strong, white, fitting into each other, which is correct when the lower incisors fit tightly into the upper ones just as two scissor blades. **Faults** – The incisors of the lower jaw are protruding (undershot) or those of the upper jaw protrude (overshot). Also, when the incisors of both jaws stand one upon another ('crackers'), for in this case the teeth wear out prematurely. Imperceptible deviations are allowed. Distemper teeth should be objected to as they hide caries; likewise when the teeth look broken or are brown. Tartar is also undesirable.

Neck:– Long, dry, muscular and sinewy, without strongly developed skin or dewlap; it should taper slightly from the chest to the head, be nicely ascending, and set on high with a well-formed nape. **Faults** – Neck short, thick with loose skin or dewlap.

Shoulders:– The shoulder-blade should be long and slanting; it should join the bone of the upper arm in the same position in the shoulder joint, as far as possible forming a right angle, in order to allow roomy movement. The withers should be well accentuated. **Faults** – Straight or loose shoulders; the former occur when the shoulder-blade is not sufficiently slanting, the latter when the elbows turn outwards.

Chest:– As large as possible, the ribs well-rounded, deep in front, reaching up to the elbow joints. **Faults** – Chest narrow, shallow with flat ribs; chest bone protruding too much.

Body:– The back straight, short and tight, the body should be as far as possible square in relation to the height; a somewhat longer back is allowed in bitches. The loins should be lightly arched and strong, the croup running fully imperceptibly into the root of the tail. The belly should be well tucked up backwards, and forming a nicely arched line with the inside of the chest. **Faults** – Saddle-back, roach-back, or when the height of the hindquarters exceeds that of the forequarters (overbuilt); too long a back, since the gait then suffers (rolling gait); the croup falling off at a slant; belly hanging down and badly showing teats in bitches.

Tail:– Of medium length, only reaching to the hocks, set on high and broad, but tapering to a point; hanging down straight at rest, slightly curved (sword-like) in excitement or in running, not carried over the back. **Faults** – Tail too long, too low set on, carried too high over the back, or curled over the back; turned sideways; broken off or docked (it is forbidden to shorten the tail to obtain the prescribed length); brush tail (when the hair on the inside is too long) is undesirable. It is forbidden to shave the tail.

Front legs:– The continuation of the elbows of the forearm must not reach the round of the chest, but must be well let down, must not appear either inwards or outwards, but should lie in equal flatness with the shoulder joint. The upper front or side – absolutely straight down to the pasterns. **Faults** – Elbows turning in or out; if turning in, their position impedes movement by rubbing against the ribs, and at the same time turns the whole lower part of the legs and causes the feet to turn outwards; if turning out, the reverse happens and the toes are forced inwards. Both these positions are at fault, but the latter does not hinder movement since it does not cause any rubbing of the elbows against the chest wall. If the forelegs stand too wide apart the feet are forced to turn inwards while in the case of the 'narrow' stand brought about by the narrow chest, the front legs incline towards each other and the toes again turn outwards. The curving of the joint of the root of the front foot is equally faulty; it points to weakness in the pasterns (soft pasterns) or in foot-roots (tarsus), and often causes flat feet and splayed toes. Swelling over the joint of the tarsus points mainly to diseases of the bone (rickets).

Hind legs:– The buttocks of the hind legs should be broad and muscular, the under-thighs long, strong and forming a not too obtuse angle with the short tarsus. Seen from behind, the hocks should appear absolutely straight, sloping neither outwards nor inwards. **Faults** – If the knee-joint is turned too far outwards, the under-thigh forces the hock inwards and the dog is then 'cow-hocked', not a nice position at all. Too broad a stand in the hocks is just as ugly, as it impedes the light movement. In profile, the well-developed hind thigh shows good angulation. A straight hind thigh is faulty, for there the under-thigh is too short and the dog is forced to keep it vertically to the straight tarsus. If the bone of the hind thighs is too long (in relation to the forelimbs), then the hind thighs are diagonally bent together, and this is not at all good.

Feet:– Roundish, turned neither inwards nor outwards. The toes should be short, highly arched and well closed, the nails short, strong and black. **Faults** – Splayed toes, hare-feet, toes turned inwards or outwards; further, the fifth toes on the hind legs placed higher (dew claw); also if the nails are too long, or light in colour.

Movement:– Fleeting, stepping out. **Faults** – Short strides which are not free; narrow or rolling gait; ambling gait.

Coat:– Very short and thick, lying close and shiny. **Faults** – Hair too long, lopped hair (due to bad feeding, worms and faulty care).

Colour:–
   (a) *Brindle Danes* – Ground colour from light golden fawn to dark golden fawn, always with well-defined black stripes. The more intense the ground colour and the stronger the stripes, the more striking is the effect. Small white patches on the chest and toes, or light eyes and nails, are not desirable. **Faults** – Silver-blue or biscuit-coloured ground colour, washed-out stripes, white streak between the eyes up to the nose, white ring on the neck, white 'socks' and white tip of tail. Danes with such markings should be excluded from winning prizes.

(b) *Fawn Danes* – Colour, fawn-golden and fawn to dark golden fawn; black mask as well as black nails are desired. The golden-fawn colour should always be preferred. **Faults** – Silver-grey, blue-grey, biscuit-fawn and dirty-fawn colour should be placed lower in the award list. For white markings, see (a) above.

(c) *Blue Danes* – The colour should be as far as possible steel blue, without any tinge of fawn or black. Lighter eyes are allowed in blue Danes. **Faults** – Fawn-blue or black-blue colour, too light or wall eyes. Regarding the white markings, see (a) above.

(d) *Black Danes* – Should be wallflower black, shiny, with dark eyes and black nails. **Faults** – Yellow-brown or blue-black colour; light or amber-coloured eyes; lightly coloured nails. Danes with too many white markings should be lower in the list of awards. Under white markings it should be noted that a white streak on the throat, spots on the chest, on toes (only up the pasterns) are allowed, but Danes with a white blaze, white ring on the neck, white 'socks' or white belly, should be debarred from winning.

(e) *Harlequins* – The ground colour should always be white, without any spots, with patches running all over the body, well-torn, irregular, wallflower black (a few small grey or brownish patches are admitted but not desired). Nose and nails should be black, but a nose with black spots or a fleshy nose are allowed. Eyes should be dark; light or two-coloured eyes are permitted but not desired. **Faults** – White ground colour with several large, black patches; bluish-grey ground colour; water-light, red or bleary eyes.

The following Danes should be excluded from winning:

1 White Danes without any black markings; albinos, as well as deaf Danes.
2 'Mantle' Harlequins, i.e. Danes having a large patch – like a mantle – running all over the body, and only the legs, neck and tip of the tail are white.
3 So-called 'Porcelain' Harlequins, i.e. Danes with mostly blue-grey, fawn or even brindle patches.

Size:– The height at the shoulder should not be under 76cm (30ins or 2.5ft) but preferably should measure about 80cm; in bitches, not under 70cm, but preferably 75cm and over.

The American Great Dane Standard

(This Standard is copyrighted by the American Kennel Club and is reproduced with their kind permission.)

1 GENERAL CONFORMATION

(a) *General Appearance*:– The Great Dane combines his distinguished appearance, dignity, strength and elegance with great size and a powerful, well-formed, smoothly muscled body. He is one of the giant breeds, but is unique in that his general conformation must be so well balanced that he never appears clumsy and is always a unit – the Apollo of dogs. He must be spirited and courageous – never timid. He is friendly and dependable. This physical and mental combination is the characteristic which gives the Great Dane the majesty possessed by no other breed. It is particularly true of this breed that there is an impression of great masculinity in dogs as compared to an impression of femininity in bitches. The male should appear more massive throughout than the bitch, with larger frame and heavier bone. In the ratio between length and height, the Great Dane should appear as square as possible. In bitches, a somewhat longer body is permissible. **Faults** – Lack of unity, timidity, bitchy dogs; poor musculature; poor bone development; out of condition; rickets; doggy bitches.

(b) *Color and Markings*:–
(I) *Brindle Danes* – Base color ranging from light golden yellow to deep golden yellow, always brindled with strong black cross-stripes; deep-black mask preferred. Black may or may not appear on the eyes, ears and a tail tip. The more intensive the base color and the more distinct the brindling, the more attractive will be the color. Small white marks at the chest and toes are not desirable. **Faults** – Brindle with too dark a base color; silver-blue and grayish-blue base color; dull (faded) brindlings; white tail tip. Black-fronted, dirty-colored brindles are not desirable.
(II) *Fawn Danes* – Light golden yellow to deep golden yellow color with a deep black mask. Black may or may not appear on the eyes, ears, and tail tip. The deep golden yellow color must always be given the preference. Small white spots at the chest and toes are not desirable. **Faults** – Yellowish-gray, bluish-yellow, grayish-blue, dirty yellow color (drab color), lack of black mask. Black-fronted, dirty-colored Fawns are not desirable.
(III) *Blue Danes* – the color must be a pure steel blue, as far as possible without any tinge of yellow, black or mouse gray. Small white marks at the chest and toes are not desirable. **Faults** – Any deviation from a pure steel-blue coloration.

(IV) *Black Danes* – Glossy black. **Faults** – Yellow-black, brown-black or blue-black. White markings, such as stripes on the chest, speckled chest and markings on the paws are permitted but not desirable.

(V) *Harlequin Danes* – Base color; pure white with black torn patches irregularly and well distributed over the entire body; pure white neck preferred. The black patches should never be large enough to give the appearance of a blanket nor so small as to give a stippled or dappled effect. (Eligible, but less desirable, are a few small gray spots; also pointings where, instead of a pure white base with black spots, there is a white base with single black hairs showing through which tend to give a salt and pepper or dirty effect.) **Faults** – White base color with a few large spots; bluish-gray pointed background.

(c) *Size*:– The male should not be less than 30 inches at the shoulders, but it is preferable that he be 32 inches or more, providing he is well proportioned to his height. The female should not be less than 28 inches at the shoulders, but it is preferable that she be 30 inches or more, providing she is well proportioned to her height.

(d) *Condition of Coat*:– The coat should be very short and thick, smooth, and glossy. **Faults** – Excessively long hair (stand-off coat); dull hair (indicating malnutrition, worms and negligent care).

(e) *Substance*:– Substance is that sufficiency of bone and muscle which rounds out a balance with the frame. **Faults** – Lightweight whippety Danes; coarse, ungainly proportioned Danes – always there should be balance.

2 MOVEMENT

(a) *Gait*:– Long, easy, springy stride with no tossing or rolling of body. The back line should move smoothly, parallel to the ground, with minimum rise and fall. The gait of the Great Dane should denote strength and power, showing good driving action in the hindquarters and good reach in front. As speed increases, there is a natural tendency for the legs to converge towards the center line of balance beneath the body and there should be no twisting in or out at the joints. **Faults** – Interference or crossing; twisting joints; short steps; stilted steps; the rear quarters should not pitch; the forelegs should not have a hackney gait. When moving rapidly, the Great Dane should not pace for the reason that it causes excessive side-to-side rolling of the body and thus reduces endurance.

(b) *Rear End (Croup, Legs, Paws)*:– The croup must be full, slightly drooping and must continue imperceptibly to the tail root. **Faults** – A croup which is too straight, a croup which slopes downward too steeply; and too narrow a croup.

Hind Legs:– The first thighs (from hip joint to knee) are broad and muscular. The second thighs (from knee to hock joint) are strong and long. Seen from the side, the angulation of the first thigh with the body, of the second thigh with the first thigh, and the pastern root with the second thigh should be very moderate, neither too straight nor too exaggerated. Seen from the rear, the hock joints appear to be perfectly straight, turned neither towards the inside nor towards the outside. **Faults** – Hind legs: soft flabby, poorly muscled thighs; cowhocks which are the result of the hock joint turning inward and the hock and rear paws turning outward; barrel legs, the result of the hock joints being too far apart; steep rear. As seen from the side, a steep rear is the result of the angles of the rear legs forming almost a straight line; over-angulation is the result of exaggerated angles between the first and second thighs and the hocks and is very conducive to weakness. The rear legs should never be too long in proportion to the front legs.

Back Paws:– Round and turned neither toward the inside nor toward the outside. Toes short, highly arched and well closed. Nails short, strong and as dark as possible. **Faults** – Spreading toes (splay foot); bent, long toes (rabbit paws); toes turned toward the outside or toward the inside. Furthermore, the fifth toe on the hind legs appearing at a higher position and with wolf's claw or spur; excessively long nails; light-colored nails.

(c) *Front End (Shoulders, Legs, Paws):*– The shoulder blades must be strong and sloping and, seen from the side, must form as nearly as possible a right angle in its articulation with the humerus (upper arm) to give a long stride. A line from the upper tip of the shoulder to the back of the elbow joint should be as nearly perpendicular as possible. Since all dogs lack a clavicle (collar bone) the ligaments and muscles holding the shoulder blade to the rib cage must be well developed, firm and secure to prevent loose shoulders. **Faults** – Steep shoulders, which occur if the shoulder blade does not slope sufficiently; overangulation; loose shoulders which occur if the Dane is flabby-muscled, or if the elbow is turned toward the outside; loaded shoulders.

Forelegs:– The upper arm should be strong and muscular. Seen from the side or front, the strong lower arms run absolutely straight to the pastern joints. Seen from the front, the forelegs and the pastern roots should form perpendicular lines to the ground. Seen from the side, the pastern root should slope only very slightly forward. **Faults** – Elbows turned toward the inside or toward the outside, the former position caused mostly by too narrow or too shallow a chest, bringing the front legs too closely together and at the same time turning the entire lower part of the leg outward; the latter position causes the front legs to spread too far apart, with the pastern roots and paws usually turned inwards. Seen from the side, a considerable bend in the pastern toward the front indicates weakness and is, in most cases, connected with stretched and spread toes (splay foot); seen from the side, a forward bow in the forearm (chair leg); an excessively knotty bulge in the front of the pastern joint.

Front Paws:– Round and turned neither toward the inside nor toward the outside. Toes short, highly arched and well closed. Nails short, strong and as dark as possible. **Faults** – Spreading toes (splay foot), bent, long toes (rabbit paws); toes turned toward the outside or toward the inside; light-colored nails.

3 HEAD

(a) *Head Conformation*:– Long, narrow, distinguished, expressive, finely chiseled, especially the part below the eyes (which means that the skull plane under and to the inner point of the eye must slope without any bony protuberance in a pleasing line to the full square jaw), with strongly pronounced stop. The masculinity of the male is very pronounced in the expression and structure of the head (this subtle difference should be evident in the dog's head through massive skull and depth of muzzle); the bitch's head may be more delicately formed. Seen from the side, the forehead must be sharply set off from the bridge of the nose. The forehead and the bridge of the nose must be straight and parallel to one another. Seen from the front, the head should appear narrow, the bridge of the nose should be as broad as possible. The cheek muscles must show slightly, but under no circumstances should they be too pronounced (cheeky). The muzzle part must have full flews and must be as blunt vertically as possible in front; the angles of the lips must be quite pronounced. The front part of the head, from the tip of the nose up to the center of the stop, should be as long as the rear part of the head from the center of the stop to the only slightly developed occiput. The head should be angular from all sides and should have definite flat planes and its dimensions should be absolutely in proportion to the general appearance of the Dane. **Faults** – Any deviation from the parallel planes of skull and foreface; too small a stop; a poorly defined stop or none at all; too narrow a nose bridge; the rear of the head spreading laterally in a wedgelike manner (wedge head); an excessively round upper head (apple head); excessively pronounced cheek musculature; pointed muzzle; loose lips hanging over the lower jaw (fluttering lips) which create an illusion of a full deep muzzle. The head should be rather shorter and distinguished than long and expressionless.

(b) *Teeth*:– Strong, well developed and clean. The incisors of the lower jaw must touch very lightly the bottoms of the inner surface of the upper incisors (scissor bite). If the front teeth of both jaws bite on top of each other, they wear down too rapidly. **Faults** – Even bite; undershot and over-shot; incisors out of line; black or brown teeth; missing teeth.

(c) *Eyes*:– Medium size, as dark as possible, with lively intelligent expression; almond-shaped eyelids, well-developed eyebrows. **Faults** – Light-colored, piercing, amber-colored, light blue to a watery blue, red or bleary eyes; eyes of different colors; eyes too far apart; Mongolian eyes; eyes with pronounced haws; eyes with excessively drooping lower eyelids. In Blue and Black Danes, lighter eyes are permitted but are not desirable. In Harlequins, the eyes should be dark. Light-colored eyes, two eyes of different color and wall-eyes are permitted but not desirable.

(d) *Nose*:– The nose must be large and in the case of brindled and 'single-colored' Danes, it must always be black. In Harlequins, the nose should be black; a black spotted nose is permitted; a pink-colored nose is not desirable.

(e) *Ears*:– Ears should be high, set not too far apart, medium in size, of moderate thickness, drooping forward close to the cheek. Top line of folded ear should be about level with the skull. **Faults** – Hanging on the side, as on a Foxhound.

Cropped Ears:– High set, not set too far apart, well pointed but always in proportion to the shape of the head and carried uniformly erect.

4 TORSO

(a) *Neck*:– The neck should be firm and clean, high set, well arched, long, muscular and sinewy. From the chest to the head it should be slightly tapering, beautifully formed, with well-developed nape. **Faults** – Short, heavy neck, pendulous throat folds (dewlaps).

(b) *Loins and Back*:– The withers form the highest part of the back which slopes downward slightly towards the loins which are imperceptibly arched and strong. The back should be short and tensely set. The belly should be well shaped and tightly muscled, and, with the rear part of the thorax, should swing in a pleasing curve (tuck-up). **Faults** – Receding back, sway back; camel or roach back; a back line which is too high at the rear; an excessively long back; poor tuck-up.

(c) *Chest*:– Chest deals with part of the thorax (rib cage) in front of the shoulders and front legs. The chest should be quite broad, deep and well muscled. **Faults** – A narrow and poorly muscled chest; strong protruding sternum (pigeon chest).

(d) *Ribs and Brisket*:– Deals with that part of the thorax back of the shoulders and front legs. Should be broad, with the ribs sprung well out from the spine and flattened at the side to allow proper movement of the shoulder extending down to the elbow joint. **Faults** – Narrow (slab-sided) rib cage; round (barrel) rib cage; shallow rib cage not reaching the elbow joint.

5 TAIL

Should start high and fairly broad, terminating slender and thin at the hock joint. At rest, the tail should fall straight. When excited or running, slightly curved (saberlike). **Faults** – A too high, or too low set tail (the tail set is governed by the slope of the croup); too long or too short a tail; tail bent too far over the back (ring tail); a tail which is curled; a twisted tail (sideways); a tail carried too high over the back (gay tail); a brush tail (hair too long on lower side). Cropping tails to desired length is forbidden.

DISQUALIFICATIONS
Danes under minimum height
White Danes without any black marks (albinos)
Merles, a solid mouse-gray color or a mouse-gray base with black or white or both color spots or white base with mouse-gray spots.
Harlequins and solid-colored Danes in which a large spot extends coatlike over the entire body so that only the legs, neck and point of the tail are white.
Brindle, Fawn, Blue and Black Danes with white forehead line, white collars, high white stockings and white bellies.
Danes with predominantly blue, gray, yellow or also brindled spots.
Any color other than those described under 'Color and Markings'.
Docked tails.
Split noses.

Approved August 10, 1976

BREEDERS' CODE OF ETHICS
as endorsed by
THE GREAT DANE CLUB OF AMERICA

There are only five recognized colors; all these basically fall into four color strains: 1. FAWN and BRINDLE, 2. HARLEQUIN and HARLEQUIN BRED BLACK, 3. BLUE and BLUE BRED BLACK, 4. BLACK. Color classifications being well founded, the Great Dane Club of America, Inc. considers it an inadvisable practice to mix color strains and it is the club's policy to adhere only to the following matings:

Color of Dane	Pedigree of Sire and Dam	Approved Breedings
1. FAWN	Four (4) Generation Pedigrees of FAWN or BRINDLE Danes *should not* CARRY BLACK, HARLE-QUIN or BLUE upon them.	1. FAWN bred to FAWN or BRINDLE only.
1. BRINDLE		1. BRINDLE bred to BRINDLE or FAWN only.
2. HARLEQUIN	Four (4) Generation Pedigrees of HARLEQUIN or HARLEQUIN BRED BLACK Danes *should not* carry FAWN, BRINDLE or BLUE upon them.	2. HARLEQUIN bred to HARLEQUIN, BLACK from HARLEQUIN BREEDING or BLACK from BLACK BREEDING only.
2. BLACK (HARLEQUIN BRED)		2. BLACK from HARLEQUIN BREEDING bred to HARLEQUIN, BLACK from HARLEQUIN BREEDING or BLACK from BLACK BREEDING only.
3. BLUE	Four (4) Generation Pedigrees of BLUE or BLUE BRED BLACK Danes *should not carry* FAWN, BRINDLE or HARLEQUIN upon them.	3. BLUE bred to BLUE, BLACK from BLUE BREEDING or BLACK from BLACK BREEDING only.
3. BLACK (BLUE BRED)		3. BLACK from BLUE BREEDING bred to BLUE, BLACK from BLUE BREEDING or BLACK from BLACK BREEDING only.

Color of Dane	Pedigree of Sire and Dam	Approved Breedings
4. BLACK (BLACK BRED)	Four (4) Generation Pedigrees of BLACK BRED Danes *should not carry* FAWN, BRINDLE, HARLE-QUIN or BLUE upon them.	4. BLACK from BLACK BREEDING bred to BLACK, BLUE or HARLEQUIN only. *(See note below.)*

Note: Black Bred Great Danes may be bred to Blacks, Blues or Harlequins only; Puppies resulting from these breedings will become Blacks or Harlequins from Harlequin breeding (category 2 above), Blacks or Blues from Blue breeding (category 3 above) or Blacks from Black Breeding (category 4 above).

It is our belief that color mixing other than that set forth above is injurious to our breed.

ALL COLORS SHALL BE PURE COLOR BRED FOR FOUR (4) GENERATIONS

Appendix I

Glossary

AFFIX	The kennel name of the breeder.
AMNIOTIC SAC	The bag in which every puppy is contained during pre-birth development and which must be removed immediately following birth in order to allow the puppy to breathe (within 30 seconds). Usually the mother of the puppy will do this.
ANAL GLANDS	Two sacs situated just inside the anal opening.
APPLE HEAD	Pronouncedly domed skull.
ASCARIDS	Type of roundworm.
ATAXIA	Unco-ordinated movements of limbs.
BARREL-RIBBED	Over-rounded rib cage.
BENCHING	Numbered stall for individual dogs at a benched show.
BITE	Describing the placement of teeth when the mouth is closed.
BLACK	Recognized breed colour.
BLOOM	In good healthy condition, particularly of coat.
BLUE	Recognized breed colour.
BOSTON	An unacceptable coat pattern appearing as a black with too much white; in fact genetically quite different from a black and related more closely to a Harlequin.
BRACE	Two Great Danes belonging to the same exhibitor.
BREED STANDARD	A written description of a particular breed published by the Kennel Club.
BRINDLE	Recognized breed colour.
BROOD BITCH	A female used for breeding.
BUTTERFLY NOSE	Not fully pigmented black.
CANKER	See otitis.
CAT FOOT	A short and compact foot with well arched toes.
CERVICAL VERTEBRAL INSTABILITY	(wobbler's syndrome, spinal stenosis). Diseases causing narrowing or compression of the spinal canal or cord.
CHALLENGE CERTIFICATE	Award given to the best exhibit of each sex at a Championship show.

CHAMPION	A dog or bitch who has been awarded three Challenge Certificates by three different judges.
CHAMPIONSHIP SHOW	A show where Challenge Certificates are available.
CHEEKY	Excessively fat cheeks.
CLEFT PALATE	Congenital defect of the roof of the mouth.
CLOSE COUPLED	Short in loin and back.
COBBY	Compact in body.
COLOSTRUM	Breast milk containing antibodies produced by the dam for about two days following the birth of her puppies.
CONFORMATION	Describing the general structure of a dog.
CONGENITAL	Defects which have been present since birth.
CRYPTORCHID	A dog whose testicles have not apparently descended into the scrotum.
CULL	To kill undesirable puppies.
CYSTITIS	Inflammation of the bladder and urinary tract.
DAM	The mother of puppies.
DEW CLAWS	Rudimentary toes with nails on the inside of legs, removed within a few days of birth.
DISH-FACED	The stop too abrupt and deep set with head planes not parallel.
DISTEMPER	Viral disease for which vaccination is available.
DISTENSION	Caused by excessive gas in the stomach.
DOWN-FACED	Not enough stop with head planes not parallel.
DOWN IN PASTERN	Weak pastern joint.
DUDLEY NOSE	A pink or brown nose.
ECLAMPSIA	A metabolic disorder of the pregnant or lactating bitch due to a deficiency of calcium.
ECTROPION	An inherited condition in which the lower eyelid is too loose and turns outwards, exposing the haw.
ELIZABETHAN COLLAR	A collar which restricts the movement of the head, so preventing a dog from interfering with wounds, etc.
ENTROPION	An inherited and painful condition in which the eyelids (upper or lower) turn in and the eyelashes rub on the eye ball.
FAWN	A recognized breed colour.
FLYAWAY EARS	Ears which are not folded so as to fall downwards and close to the head.
FLYER	Used to describe a young dog who is winning well at shows.
GAIT	Movement of a dog.
GAY TAIL	A tail carried too high.
GENES	Units of inheritance.
GESTATION	The period from conception to birth of puppies, averaging 63 days.
HACKNEY GAIT	Lifting the front feet too high.

HARDPAD	See distemper.
HARE FOOT	A long and flat foot.
HARLEQUIN	Recognized breed colour.
HAW	Inner lining of the lower eyelid.
HEAT	See season.
HEIGHT	Measured from the ground to the withers.
HEPATITIS	A viral disease for which vaccination is available.
HIP DISPLASIA (H.D.)	Abnormal ball and socket joint of the hips, varying in degree.
HYPERMOTILITY	A condition which accounts for 90% of diarrhoea in dogs.
IN BREEDING	The mating of very closely related dogs (incestuous matings).
INCONTINENCE	The inability to control the flow of urine or bowel movements.
IN WHELP	Describing a pregnant bitch.
JUNIOR	Describing an exhibit not exceeding 18 months of age (in practice 12–18 months of age).
KENNEL COUGH	Infection of the upper respiratory tract, very contagious, vaccination partly effective.
KNUCKLE OVER	Forelegs that buckle forward at the pastern.
LEGGY	Describing a dog whose legs are too long.
LEPTOSPIROSIS	Bacterial infections for which vaccinations are available.
LINE BREEDING	The mating of distantly related dogs.
LIPPY	Describing a dog with heavy or pendulous lips.
LITTER	A collection of puppies born at one whelping.
LOADED SHOULDERS	Shoulders with heavy muscling.
MANGE	Parasitic mites causing skin infections.
MASK	The dark shading of the foreface (muzzle).
MASTITIS	Inflammation of the breasts.
MERLE	A coat pattern, blue/grey background with black patches. This colour carries lethal or undesirable genes and in Great Danes is a mismark.
METABOLIC	The biological balance within a living body.
METRITIS	Inflammation of the uterus.
MISMARK	Colour deviation which is unacceptable in show dogs.
MONORCHID	Male dogs with only one descended testicle.
NICTITATING MEMBRANE	The third eyelid.
NEPHRITIS	Inflammation of the kidneys.
OESTRUS	See season.
OUT AT ELBOW	Usually resulting from incorrect shoulders causing elbows to wave outwards when on the move.
OUTCROSS	The mating of totally unrelated dogs.
OTITIS	Inflammation of the ear.
PACING	Moving front and hind legs on the same side of the

	body in unison.
PADDLING	Throwing legs outwards rather than straight in front when gaiting.
PARATHYROIDS	Four small glands in the neck of the dog, located in close proximity to the thyroid. Parathyroids secrete a hormone important in calcium and bone metabolism.
PART BREEDING TERMS	A written agreement between a breeder and another person regarding the offspring of the said dog or bitch.
PARVO VIRUS	A viral infection for which vaccinations are available.
PEDIGREE	A written record of a dog's ancestors.
PHANTOM PREGNANCY	A bitch showing signs of being in whelp, when in reality she is not.
PLACENTA	The 'afterbirth' of a puppy.
PROGENY	The offspring.
PUPPY	A young dog not over 12 months of age.
PUPPY FARMS	Retail outlets for many breeds of dogs. Reputable breeders do not supply such places.
QUARANTINE	A period of confinement in a specially designated kennel for all dogs imported from abroad, to prevent the spread of infection.
QUARTERS	A broad term referring to either the front or rear assembly of a dog. Forequarters, hindquarters.
RABIES	A lethal infection of animals and man (the main reason for quarantining imported dogs).
RINGTAIL	The end of the tail curls right round so as to form a ring.
RINGWORM	A skin disease caused by fungus.
ROACH BACK	A dog whose topline has a humped appearance.
ROUNDWORM	An internal parasitic worm.
SCHEDULE	A programme of events and classes for a forthcoming dog show.
SEASON	The period during which a bitch may be mated.
SERVICE	Sometimes used to describe a dog mating a bitch.
SHELLY	A narrow body, lacking substance.
SIRE	The father of puppies.
SLAB-SIDED	A rib cage with lack of roundness.
SNIPY	A foreface that is too narrow.
SPRING OF RIB	A well developed rib cage indicating good lung and heart capacity.
STRAIGHT-IN SHOULDER	Incorrect shoulder angulation.
STUD	A dog used to father puppies.
SUPERCILLARY ARCHES	Bony structure above the eyes.
SWAY BACK	A dipping back falling below a level topline.
TAPEWORM	Internal parasitic worm.
TEAM	Three or more exhibits belonging to the same exhibitor.

THROATY	Too much loose skin on the throat.
TIE	Describing the union of a dog and bitch during mating.
TORSION	The twisting of an organ.
TOXAEMIA	Poisons in the body.
WALL-EYE	An unpigmented iris, allowable in Harlequins only.
WHELP	A young puppy.
WHELPING	A bitch is said to be whelping when she is giving birth.
WORKING GROUP	Group classification under which the Great Dane is shown at present.

Appendix II

Gestation Table

Served Jan.	Whelps March	Served Feb.	Whelps April	Served March	Whelps May	Served April	Whelps June	Served May	Whelps July	Served June	Whelps Aug.	Served July	Whelps Sept.	Served Aug.	Whelps Oct.	Served Sept.	Whelps Nov.	Served Oct.	Whelps Dec.	Served Nov.	Whelps Jan.	Served Dec.	Whelps Feb.
1	5	1	5	1	3	1	3	1	3	1	3	1	2	1	3	1	3	1	3	1	3	1	2
2	6	2	6	2	4	2	4	2	4	2	4	2	3	2	4	2	4	2	4	2	4	2	3
3	7	3	7	3	5	3	5	3	5	3	5	3	4	3	5	3	5	3	5	3	5	3	4
4	8	4	8	4	6	4	6	4	6	4	6	4	5	4	6	4	6	4	6	4	6	4	5
5	9	5	9	5	7	5	7	5	7	5	7	5	6	5	7	5	7	5	7	5	7	5	6
6	10	6	10	6	8	6	8	6	8	6	8	6	7	6	8	6	8	6	8	6	8	6	7
7	11	7	11	7	9	7	9	7	9	7	9	7	8	7	9	7	9	7	9	7	9	7	8
8	12	8	12	8	10	8	10	8	10	8	10	8	9	8	10	8	10	8	10	8	10	8	9
9	13	9	13	9	11	9	11	9	11	9	11	9	10	9	11	9	11	9	11	9	11	9	10
10	14	10	14	10	12	10	12	10	12	10	12	10	11	10	12	10	12	10	12	10	12	10	11
11	15	11	15	11	13	11	13	11	13	11	13	11	12	11	13	11	13	11	13	11	13	11	12
12	16	12	16	12	14	12	14	12	14	12	14	12	13	12	14	12	14	12	14	12	14	12	13
13	17	13	17	13	15	13	15	13	15	13	15	13	14	13	15	13	15	13	15	13	15	13	14
14	18	14	18	14	16	14	16	14	16	14	16	14	15	14	16	14	16	14	16	14	16	14	15
15	19	15	19	15	17	15	17	15	17	15	17	15	16	15	17	15	17	15	17	15	17	15	16
16	20	16	20	16	18	16	18	16	18	16	18	16	17	16	18	16	18	16	18	16	18	16	17
17	21	17	21	17	19	17	19	17	19	17	19	17	18	17	19	17	19	17	19	17	19	17	18
18	22	18	22	18	20	18	20	18	20	18	20	18	19	18	20	18	20	18	20	18	20	18	19
19	23	19	23	19	21	19	21	19	21	19	21	19	20	19	21	19	21	19	21	19	21	19	20
20	24	20	24	20	22	20	22	20	22	20	22	20	21	20	22	20	22	20	22	20	22	20	21
21	25	21	25	21	23	21	23	21	23	21	23	21	22	21	23	21	23	21	23	21	23	21	22
22	26	22	26	22	24	22	24	22	24	22	24	22	23	22	24	22	24	22	24	22	24	22	23
23	27	23	27	23	25	23	25	23	25	23	25	23	24	23	25	23	25	23	25	23	25	23	24
24	28	24	28	24	26	24	26	24	26	24	26	24	25	24	26	24	26	24	26	24	26	24	25
25	29	25	29	25	27	25	27	25	27	25	27	25	26	25	27	25	27	25	27	25	27	25	26
26	30	26	30	26	28	26	28	26	28	26	28	26	27	26	28	26	28	26	28	26	28	26	27
27	31	27	1	27	29	27	29	27	29	27	29	27	28	27	29	27	29	27	29	27	29	27	28
28	1	28	2	28	30	28	30	28	30	28	30	28	29	28	30	28	30	28	30	28	30	28	1
29	2	29	3	29	31	29	1	29	31	29	31	29	30	29	31	29	1	29	1	29	31	29	2
30	3			30	1	30	2	30	1	30	1	30	1	30	1	30	2	30	2	30	1	30	3
31	4			31	2			31	2			31	2	31	2			31	2			31	4

Appendix III   Sample Pedigree

Pedigree of .... CHENEY TRULY SCRUMPTIOUS ....

PARENTS	Grandparents	GreatGrandparents
SIRE THE VINDICATOR OF CHENEY	**SIRE** CHAMPION THE CONTENDER OF DICARL	**SIRE** CHAMPION THE WEIGHTLIFTER OF DICARL
		DAM ENDROMA LUCKY LOO
	DAM KEMPSHOTT GEMINI GIRL OF DONCERO	**SIRE** PEER GYNT OF HELMLAKE OF KEMPSHOTT
		DAM OLDMANOR MAYMINX OF KEMPSHOTT
DAM SALPETRA BIG BESS OF CHENEY	**SIRE** LINCOLN'S WINSTEAD VON RASEAC (USA IMPORT)	**SIRE** AMERICAN CHAMPI VON RASEAC'S TYBO O'LORCAIN
		DAM AMERICAN CHAMPI VON RASEAC'S QUITE A GAL
	DAM CHAMPION SHERRY OF SHERAIN OF SALPETRA	**SIRE** SHERAIN SAUL
		DAM GOWERFIELD GARROD

We certify that to the best of our knowledge this Pedigree is c

eed GREAT DANE **Colour** FAWN **Date of Registration** 4.7.1985

x FEMALE **Breeder** DOWN & MACDONALD **Stud Book No.**

te of Birth 19.3.1985 **Kennel Club No.** K3854701K10 **Owner** BREEDERS

GreatGreatGrandparents	GreatGreatGreatGrandparents	
CHAMPION DICARL THE HEAVYWEIGHT	SIRE	CH. GOWERFIELD GALESTORM OF AVSDAINE
	DAM	DICARL TARDUB
CHAMPION DICARL THE LIONESS OF JAFRAK	SIRE	CH. SIMBA OF HELMLAKE
	DAM	DICARL TARBABY
MY LUCK OF OLDMANOR	SIRE	CH. OLDMANOR PIONEER OF DANEII
	DAM	CH. MUFFETTEE OF OLDMANOR
CHAMPION LAVENETTE OF ENDROMA	SIRE	CH. OLDMANOR PIONEER OF DANEII
	DAM	MERMAID OF OLDMANOR
CHAMPION SIMBA OF HELMLAKE	SIRE	CH. FERGUS OF CLAUSENTUM
	DAM	CH. MISS FREEDOM OF MERROWLEA
FRANNY OF CLAUSENTUM	SIRE	ROBIN OF CLAUSENTUM
	DAM	AMBER OF CLAUSENTUM
CHAMPION MELETALYON OF OLDMANOR	SIRE	CH. TELAMAN OF MOONSFIELD
	DAM	CH. MELETA OF OLDMANOR
CHAMPION MISS MONICA OF OLDMANOR	SIRE	CH. OLDMANOR PIONEER OF DANEII
	DAM	MISS BAMFORD OF OLDMANOR
AMERICAN CHAMPION SUNRIDGE'S CHIEF JUSTICE	SIRE	AM. CH. MOUNTDANIA'S TIMBER
	DAM	AM. CH. TROY'S WENDY OF HEARTH HILL
AMERICAN CHAMPION VON ?ASEAC'S QUINTESSENCE	SIRE	GREAT CAESAR'S GHOST VON RASEAC
	DAM	CAMEO LILABET OF JASON
GREAT CAESAR'S GHOST VON RASEAC	SIRE	AM. CH. DANA'S ZEUS OF QUINDANE
	DAM	CAESAR'S LORELET VON OVERCUP
CAMEO'S LILABET OF JASON	SIRE	AM. CH. OVERCUP'S JASON SACERDOTES
	DAM	BODON'S CAMEO GIRL VON FURY
CHAMPION WALKMYLL CASTOR OF CLAUSENTUM	SIRE	CH. FERGUS OF CLAUSENTUM
	DAM	JENNIFER OF CLAUSENTUM
SERENA OF SHERAIN	SIRE	TRUE CHANCE OF MOONSFIELD
	DAM	ANN DARLING OF ANCHOLME
AEDOR OF GOWERFIELD	SIRE	SHERAIN TRADITION OF MOONSFIELD
	DAM	CH. GOWERFIELD CANDYCARESS OF AYSDAINE
?ATCHMEAD SERENADE	SIRE	CH. PADDY OF DANEMORE
	DAM	PRUNELLA OF NIGHTSGIFT

M.DOWN : B. MacDonald   MAY 1985

Appendix IV

Sample Diet Sheet for Puppies

Beta 2 Puppy is a carefully balanced food, specially formulated for rearing puppies. It contains an ideal balance of protein, carbohydrates, vitamins, minerals, trace elements, etc. Under no circumstances should you upset the balance by adding meat or vitamins, with the exception of Vitamin C. Beta 2 Puppy should be used until your puppy is 9 months old, preferably 18–24 months old. If you have any problems regarding feeding, then please ask a veterinary surgeon.

Diet for a puppy of 8 weeks
9 am – 4 ozs Beta 2 Puppy soaked in
        warm water for about 15 minutes.
1 pm – same as 9 am.
5 pm – same as 9 am.
9 pm – same as 9 am.
Please give each day 1 gram of Vitamin C.

MOST IMPORTANT Ensure that there is a supply of clean fresh drinking water available at all times.

Each puppy is an individual and their needs vary. Obviously the above amount should be increased slightly each week, and increases should be made on a gradual basis over each meal. As a guide, stools should be well formed: if they are soft or watery it is possible that too much food is being given. If this happens reduce the amount of food offered. Your aim should be to have a well covered, but on no account fat, puppy. He should be active and not lethargic. You may reduce the number of feeds to 3 per day when your puppy is about 16 weeks old and to 2 feeds per day when he is about 9 months old.

DO NOT FEED TO APPETITE

Appendix V

Colour codes

F = Fawn   Be = Blue
Br = Brindle   H = Harlequin
Bk = Black

Post-War Champions

YEAR	NAME	SEX	BIRTH	COL	SIRE	DAM	OWNER	BREEDER
1945	Nil							
1946	Nil							
1947	Nil							
1948	Juan of Winome	D	24-6-44	F	Bafflino of Blendon	Brindle Lady of Winome	Mrs E.C. Rowberry	Capt. & Mrs Rowberry
1948	Royalism of Ouborough	D	15-7-45	F	Raffles of Ouborough	Rezhitsa of Ouborough	Mr J.V. Rank	Mr J.V. Rank
1948	Bon Adventure of Barvae	B	10-1-46	F	Rebellion of Ouborough	Bridesmaid of Barvae	Mrs G.M. Clayton	Mrs G.M. Clayton
1949	Frost of the Wideskies	D	8-1-46	H	Storm of the Wideskies	Mist of the Wideskies	Miss M. Lomas	Miss M. Lomas
1949	Jillida of Winome	B	13-5-46	F	Rebellion of Ouborough	Juno of Winome	Mrs E.C. Rowberry	Mrs E.C. Rowberry
1949	Raet of Ouborough	B	15-4-46	Br	Ch. Royalism of Ouborough	Ch. Ryot of Ouborough	Mr J.V. Rank	Mrs C.R. Robb
1949	Rusa of Ouborough	B	4-3-45	F	Rebellion of Ouborough	Rola of Ouborough	Mr J.V. Rank	Mr. J.V. Rank
1949	Ryot of Ouborough	B	4-3-45	Br	Rebellion of Ouborough	Rola of Ouborough	Mrs C.R. Robb	Mr J.V. Rank
1950	Basra of Bringtonhill	D	23-6-44	F	Hyperion of Ladymeade	Black Beauty of Brington	Mrs R.W. Ennals	Mrs R.W. Ennals
1950	Revert of Ouborough	D	19-10-45	F	Rilon Wilverly Romeo	Rubye of Ouborough	Mrs E.J. Allen	Mr J.V. Rank

YEAR	NAME	SEX	BIRTH	COL	SIRE	DAM	OWNER	BREEDER
1950	Dawnlight of Ickford	D	28-11-47	F	Ch. Royalism of Ouborough	Radiance of Ladymeade	Mrs M.S. Laming	Mrs M.S. Laming
1950	Rivolet of Ouborough	D	26-3-46	F	Rebellion of Ouborough	Jessica of Winome	Mr W.G. Siggers	Mr W. Thorp
1950	Banshee of Bringtonhill	B	9-5-47	Bk	Bahram of Bringtonhill	Black Beauty of Brington	Mrs R.W. Ennals	Mrs R.W. Ennals
1950	Jezebel of Winome	B	13-9-47	F	Blendons Fingards King of Kings	Juno of Winome	Mrs R.D.S. Main	Mrs E.C. Rowberry
1950	Rindel of Ouborough	B	15-4-47	Br	Ch. Royalism of Ouborough	Ch. Ryot of Ouborough	Mr J.V. Rank	Mrs C.R. Robb
1951	Jeep of Winome	D	13-9-47	F	Blendons Fingards King of Kings	Juno of Winome	Mrs E.C. Rowberry	Mrs E.C. Rowberry
1951	Penelope of Alderwasley	B	15-8-47	Br	Rambert of Ouborough	Bitter Sweet of Barvae	Mr & Mrs A. Perry	Mrs M. Perry
1952	Cloud of the Wideskies	D	6-4-45	H	Storm of the Wideskies	Dusk of the Wideskies	Miss M. Lomas	Miss M. Lomas
1952	Anndae Royal Light of Ickford	D	28-11-47	F	Ch. Royalism of Ouborough	Radiance of Ladymeade	Mr J.W.L. McKee	Mrs M.S. Laming
1952	Bonhomie of Blendon	D	23-12-49	Br	Bonheur of Blendon	Jhelum of Winome	Miss H.M. Osborn	Miss H.M. Osborn
1952	Deucher of Rynallen	D	1-1-48	F	Ch. Royalism of Ouborough	Reck of Ouborough	Miss L.B. Farquharson	Miss L.B. Farquharson
1952	Relate of Ouborough	D	21-2-50	F	Relec of Ouborough	Ch. Raet of Ouborough	Mr J.V. Rank	Mr J.V. Rank
1952	Baffleur of Blendon	B	17-3-48	F	Blendons Fingards King of Kings	Baflette of Blendon	Mr Gordon Stewart	Miss H.M. Osborn
1952	Berynthia of Blendon	B	17-3-48	F	Blendons Fingards King of Kings	Baflette of Blendon	Miss H.M. Osborn	Miss H.M. Osborn
1952	Rhagodia of Ouborough	B	16-8-48	F	Ch. Royalism of Ouborough	Blenda Flicka von Langenhof	Mr J.V. Rank	Mr A.M. Kuhn
1953	Elch Edler of Ouborough	D	26-4-51	F	Kalandus of Ouborough	Ch. Raet of Ouborough	Mr W.G. Siggers	Mr J.V. Rank

YEAR	NAME	SEX	BIRTH	COL	SIRE	DAM	OWNER	BREEDER
1953	Marfre Modern Ransom	D	7-8-49	F	Ch. Royalism of Ouborough	Bambi of Ouborough	Mrs M. Jones	Mrs J. McArthur Rank
1953	Imogen of Oldmanor	B	27-1-50	Br	Oldmanor Joyalism of Winome	Dainty of Oldmanor	Rev. & Mrs J.G. Davies	Mrs C. & Miss O. Russell
1953	Tandye of Moonsfield	B	5-9-48	F	Ch. Royalism of Ouborough	Tango of Moonsfield	Mrs E.M. Harrild	Mrs E.M. Harrild
1953	Vegar of Ouborough	B	23-2-47	Br	Marfre Danilo	Rezhitsa of Ouborough	Mrs I.B. Jones	Mr J.V. Rank
1954	Boniface of Blendon	D	1-6-51	F	Ch. Bonhomie of Blendon	Berynthia of Blendon	Miss H.M. Osborn	Miss H.M. Osborn
1954	Festival of Ouborough	D	19-9-50	F	Kalandus of Ouborough	Ch. Raet of Ouborough	Mr L.E. Jacobs	Mr J.V. Rank
1955	Blaciack of Bringtonhill	D	11-4-51	Bk	Ch. Dawnlight of Ickford	Ch. Banshee of Bringtonhill	Mrs R.W. Ennals	Mrs R.W. Ennals
1955	Brin Cezar of Barvae	D	2-12-50	Br	Brindsley of Blendon	Ch. Bon Adventure of Barvae	Mr R. Wilkinson	Mrs G.M. Clayton
1955	Bronx of Blendon	D	21-7-48	F	Brandy of Blendon	Deborah of Blundell	Miss. H.M. Osborn	Mr J.B. Scuffman
1955	Racketeer of Foxbar	D	5-5-50	Br	Ch. Royalism of Ouborough	Ch. Ryot of Ouborough	Mrs C.R. Robb	Mrs C.R. Robb
1955	Marfre Modern Miss	B	26-9-51	F	Ch. Marfre Modern Ransom	Ch. Rindel of Ouborough	Mrs M.S. Jones	Mrs C.R. Robb
1955	Rhapsody of Foxbar	B	26-9-51	Br	Ch. Marfre Modern Ransom	Ch. Rindel of Ouborough	Mrs E.M. Harrild	Mrs C.R. Robb
1956	Challenger of Clausentum	D	15-6-53	F	Ch. Bronx of Blendon	Claire of Clausentum	Mrs H.A. & Miss J.M. Lanning	Mrs H.A. & Miss J.M. Lanning
1956	Baroness of Coxdown	B	19-4-53	F	Ch. Elch Edler of Ouborough	Cleopatra of Coxdown	Miss D.V. Harding	Miss D.V. Harding
1956	Flambonetta of Billi	B	22-1-53	F	Ch. Bronx of Blendon	Flamusine of Billil	Miss J.I. Cameron	Mrs L. Isaac
1956	Surtees of Leesthorphill	D	8-9-50	H	Ch. Cloud of the Wideskies	Snow of the Wideskies	Mrs J. Kelly	Mrs J. Kelly

YEAR	NAME	SEX	BIRTH	COL	SIRE	DAM	OWNER	BREEDER
1957	Benign of Blendon	D	14–4–54	Br	Ch. Bronx of Blendon	Bethanie of Blendon	Miss H.M. Osborn	Miss H.M. Osborn
1957	Barilla of Ashthorpe	B	30–10–52	F	Aurorus of Rorydale	Khumbirgram Attraction	Mrs W. Atkin	Mrs J. Drinkwater
1957	Rhythm of Foxbar	B	26–9–51	Br	Ch. Marfre Modern Ransom	Ch. Rindel of Ouborough	Mr W.G. Siggers	Mrs C.R. Robb
1958	Telluson of Moonsfield	D	2–6–56	F	Tellus of Moonsfield	Merrie of Merrowlea	Mrs E.M. Harrild	Mr W. Page
1958	Bequest of Blendon	D	12–6–55	Br	Ch. Bonhomie of Blendon	Ch. Imogen of Oldmanor	Miss H.M. Osborn	Rev. & Mrs J.G. Davies
1958	Dawn of the Wideskies	B	3–2–54	H	Halo of the Wideskies	Madonna of the Wideskies	Mr L. Rose	Miss M. Lomas
1958	Enchantment of Yalding	B	18–4–54	F	Ch. Boniface of Blendon	Lady Suzette of Miriel	Mrs E. Cadbury-Brown	Mrs M.W. Hampshire
1958	Minuet of Oldmanor	B	12–6–55	F	Ch. Bonhomie of Blendon	Ch. Imogen of Oldmanor	Rev. & Mrs J.G. Davies	Rev. & Mrs J.G. Davies
1959	Bonifleur of Blendon	B	5–8–57	F	Bonifino of Blendon	Bronfleur of Blendon	Miss H.M. Osborn	Miss H.M. Osborn
1959	Squire of Ridgedaine	D	29–10–54	F	Ch. Elch Edler of Ouborough	Rux of Ouborough	Miss J.P. Prentis	Miss J.P. Prentis
1959	Isobelle of Ashtrees	B	10–5–54	F	Ch. Elch Edler of Ouborough	Modern Ranger	Mr J. & Miss L.E. Jackson	Mr J. & Miss L.E. Jackson
1959	Marquise of Hornsgreen	B	8–10–55	Bk	Bahni of Bringtonhill	Newtonregis Belle	Major & Mrs M.P. McFarland	Mrs N. Rowe
1959	Tellus of Moonsfield	D	29–7–54	F	Ch. Elch Edler of Ouborough	Ch. Rhapsody of Foxbar	Mrs E.M. Harrild	Mrs E.M. Harrild
1959	Bonaida of Barvae	B	15–9–54	Br	Vulpus von Schloss Dellwig	Bon Viva of Barvae	Mr & Mrs M.S. Green	Mrs G.M. Clayton
1959	Bel Ami of Nightsgift	D	7–3–55	F	Ch. Bonhomie of Blendon	Ch. Flambonetta of Bilil	Miss J.C. Cameron	Miss J.C. Cameron
1960	Todhunter of Moonsfield	D	12–10–58	F	Ch. Telluson of Moonsfield	Taral of Moonsfield	Mrs M.S. Jones	Mrs E.M. Harrild

YEAR	NAME	SEX	BIRTH	COL	SIRE	DAM	OWNER	BREEDER
1960	Busaco of Blendon	D	5-9-57	Br	Bonifino of Blendon	Bronfleur of Blendon	Miss H.M. Osborn	Miss H.M. Osborn
1960	Sutton of Leesthorphill	D	14-5-56	H	Ch. Surtees of Leesthorphill	Sucan of Leesthorphill	Mrs J. Kelly	Mrs J. Kelly
1960	Moyra of of Oldmanor	B	1-11-56	Br	Oldmanor Brand of Bringtonhill	Ch. Imogen of Oldmanor	Rev. & Mrs J.G. Davies	Rev. & Mrs J.G. Davies
1961	Banquet of Blendon	D	31-3-58	Br	Ch. Bequest of Blendon	Carousel of Clounaye	Mrs N. Hanson	Mrs B. Sherman
1961	Blendon Apollo of Coldash	D	5-1-58	F	Ch. Boniface of Blendon	Vels Vanity	Miss H.M. Osborn	Mrs A.B. Pope
1961	Hampton of Ridgedaine	D	26-11-55	F	Brinsley of Barvae	Cinnamon of Ridgedaine	Miss J.P. Prentis	Miss J.P. Prentis
1961	Hyperbole of Ouborough	D	7-11-58	F	Sabre of Horsebridge	Etfa of Ouborough	Mr W.G. Siggers	Mr W.G. Siggers
1961	Telton of Moonsfield	D	26-4-56	F	Ch. Tellus of Moonsfield	Twinstar of Moonsfield	Mrs E.M. Harrild	Mrs E.M. Harrild
1961	Minuet Miss of Oldmanor	B	24-12-57	F	Ch. Bequest of Blendon	Ch. Minuet of Oldmanor	Rev. & Mrs J.G. Davies	Rev. & Mrs J.G. Davies
1962	Benison of Blendon	D	3-12-58	F	Ch. Benign of Blendon	Bronfleur of Blendon	Miss H.M. Osborn	Miss H.M. Osborn
1962	Saturn of Nightsgift	D	7-3-60	F	Benjamin of Newtonregis	Bonetta of Nightsgift	Miss J. Cameron	Miss J. Cameron
1962	Survey of Leesthorphill	D	15-2-59	H	Ch. Surtees of Leesthorphill	Nugget of Gold of the Limes	Mrs J. Kelly	Mrs J. Kelly
1962	Seranda of Leesthorphill	B	17-9-57	H	Seagull of Leesthorphill	Nugget of Gold of the Limes	Mrs J. Kelly	Mrs J. Kelly
1962	Tapestry of Moonsfield	B	24-3-58	Br	Ch. Bequest of Blendon	Twinstar of Moonsfield	Mr H.V. Harrild	Mrs E.M. Harrild
1962	Surcelle of Leesthorphill	B	15-2-59	H	Ch. Surtees of Leesthorphill	Nugget of Gold of the Limes	Mrs J. Kelly	Mrs J. Kelly
1962	Penruddock Eslilda	B	10-10-56	Br	Flamatelot of Billil	Penruddock Esmeralda	Mrs D.K.F. Peck	Mrs D.K.F. Peck

YEAR	NAME	SEX	BIRTH	COL	SIRE	DAM	OWNER	BREEDER
1963	Archie of Arranton	D	2–12–60	F	Arab of Arranton	Kerensa of Ashthorpe	Mr & Mrs S.A. Green	Mr A. Wildman
1963	Malloy of Merrowlea	D	12–12–59	F	My Choice of Merrowlea	Marilon of Merrowlea	Miss P.M. Rossiter	Mrs J. Toye
1963	Moyalism of Oldmanor	D	4–10–59	Br	Oldmanor Tattoo of Moonsfield	Ch. Moyra of Oldmanor	Rev. & Mrs J.G. Davies	Rev. & Mrs J.G. Davies
1963	Goldendale Gay of Merrowlea	B	3–6–57	F	Ch. Squire of Ridgedaine	Genevieve of Goldendale	Capt. & Mrs E.J. Hutton	Mrs G. Harrison
1963	Soraya of Nightsgift	B	20–2–59	F	Ch. Tellus of Moonsfield	Ch. Flambonetta of Billil	Miss J. Cameron	Miss J. Cameron
1964	Milady of Hornsgreen	B	24–8–59	Bk	Black Banner of Blendon	Ch. Marquise of Hornsgreen	Mr D. Hewlett	Major & Mrs M.P. MacFarland
1964	Bullington Corneille	D	11–2–61	F	Bullington Algenon of Arranton	Flamunity of Billil	Mr & Mrs Bryn-Jones	Mrs J. Makin
1964	Telaman of Moonsfield	D	23–1–62	F	Ch. Telluson of Moonsfield	Taral of Moonsfield	Mrs E.M. Harrild	Mrs E.M. Harrild
1964	Anne of Arranton	B	2–12–60	F	Arab of Arranton	Kerensa of Ashthorpe	Mr & Mrs S.A. Green	Mr A. Wildman
1964	Surice of Leesthorphill	B	11–1–52	H	Ch. Sutton of Leesthorphill	Ch. Survey of Leesthorphill	Mrs J. Kelly	Mrs J. Kelly
1965	Arex of Arranton	D	4–2–62	F	Arab of Arranton	Kerensa of Ashthorpe	Mr & Mrs S.A. Green	Mr A. Wildman
1965	Merrymonk of Merrowlea	D	2–10–61	F	Ch. Malloy of Merrowlea	Ch. Goldendale Gay of Merrowlea	Capt. & Mrs E.J. Hutton	Capt. E.J. Hutton
1965	Amalia of Arranton	B	17–2–60	Br	Oldmanor Tattoo of Moonsfield	Aida of Arranton	Mr & Mrs S.A. Green	Mrs L. Edsall
1965	Billil Tres Bon of Moonsfield	B	30–7–61	F	Ch. Telluson of Moonsfield	Tellona of Moonsfield	Mrs L. Isaac	Mrs E.M. Harrild
1965	Walkmyll Moonyean of Edzell	B	15–11–62	F	Oldmanor Tattoo of Moonsfield	Aida of Arranton	Mrs F.C. Lewis	Mrs L. Edsall
1965	Tayntemead Tamsee of Moonsfield	B	20–2–60	Br	Vanburgh of Clartay	Dunbracken Gardrum Morag	Mrs A.E. Spencer	Miss E. Niven

YEAR	NAME	SEX	BIRTH	COL	SIRE	DAM	OWNER	BREEDER
1965	Hatchmead Pericles of Nightsgift	D	13-6-61	F	Ch. Saturn of Nightsgift	Ch. Soraya of Nightsgift	Mrs J. Thomas	Miss J. Cameron
1966	Mason of Edzell	D	15-6-63	Br	Arrand of Arranton	Amber Light of Ancholme	Mr & Mrs P.V.K. Edsall	Mrs Atkins
1966	Moretime of Merrowlea	D	21-2-61	F	Sabre of Horsebridge	Musical Lyric of Merrowlea	Mr A.S. Cormack	Mrs E.M. Nobbs
1966	Mr Softee of Merrowlea	D	18-10-62	F	Ch. Malloy of Merrowlea	Ch. Goldendale Gay of Merrowlea	Capt. & Mrs E.J. Hutton	Capt. & Mrs E.J. Hutton
1966	Meleta of Oldmanor	B	4-5-62	F	Ch. Moyalism of Oldmanor	Minuet Maid of Oldmanor	Rev. & Mrs J.G. Davies	Rev. & Mrs J.G. Davies
1966	Sulia of Leesthorphill	B	11-8-64	H	Surrel of Leesthorphill	Sequence of Leesthorphill	Mrs J. Kelly	Mrs J. Kelly
1966	Madame of Merrowlea	B	18-11-60	F	Sultan of Ridgedaine	My Fair Lady of Merrowlea	Capt. & Mrs E.J. Hutton	Mr F.G. Kinch
1966	Beechfield Buxom Wench of Texall	B	27-1-64	F	Oldmanor Brand of Bringtonhill	Caribbean Queen	Mrs B. Kirkman	Mr H.V. Anderson
1967	Merry Deal of Merrowlea	D	18-10-62	F	Ch. Malloy of Merrowlea	Ch. Goldendale Gay of Merrowlea	Capt. & Mrs E.J. Hutton	Capt. & Mrs E.J. Hutton
1967	Buscilla of Blendon	B	11-10-63	Br	Ch. Busaco of Blendon	Banksia of Blendon	Miss H.M. Osborn	Miss H.M. Osborn
1967	Comtessa Fiona of Ouborough	B	23-6-63	Br	Quantas of Ouborough	Vila of Ouborough	Mr W.G. Siggers	Mr W.G. Siggers
1967	Oldmanor Pioneer of Daneii	D	26-2-64	F	Ch. Moyalism of Oldmanor	Mysore of Oldmanor	Rev. & Mrs J.G. Davies	Mr V. Fones
1967	Miss Fancy Free of Merrowlea	B	18-10-62	F	Ch. Malloy of Merrowlea	Ch. Goldendale Gay of Merrowlea	Capt. & Mrs E.J. Hutton	Capt. & Mrs E.J. Hutton
1967	My Mink of Merrowlea	B	26-7-62	F	Sabre of Horsebridge	Melia of Merrowlea	Mrs D.A. Oliver	Mrs D.A. Oliver
1967	Sawspitsville	D	26-4-64	F	Ch. Todhunter of Moonsfield	Benizora of Blendon	Mr J.W. Ellyatt	Major & Mrs Smither
1967	Clausentum Fenton of Fenbridge	D	23-9-65	F	Ch. Arex of Arranton	Jayessem Janice	Mrs H.A. & Miss J.M. Lanning	Mr W. Bishop

YEAR	NAME	SEX	BIRTH	COL	SIRE	DAM	OWNER	BREEDER
1967	Struth of Bringtonhill	D	29-11-66	F	Ch. Telaman of Moonsfield	Solitaire of Bringtonhill	Mrs R. W. Ennals	Mrs R. W. Ennals
1968	Astrid of Arranton	D	6-6-64	F	Ch. Telaman of Moonsfield	Ch. Anne of Arranton	Mrs J. Laing	Mr & Mrs A. Green
1968	Bencaross Beau Brummel	D	3-1-66	F	Ch. Oldmanor Pioneer of Daneii	Ch. Try Again of Moonsfield	Mrs Ann Danby	Mr & Mrs B. Round
1968	Lavenette of Endroma	B	29-6-66	F	Ch. Oldmanor Pioneer of Daneii	Mermaid of Oldmanor	Mr & Mrs P. Russell	Owners
1968	Melba Messenger of Oldmanor	D	21-6-65	F	Ch. Oldmanor Pioneer of Daneii	Mimelba of Oldmanor	Mrs V.N. Forrest	Rev. & Mrs J.G. Davies
1968	Mighty Fine of Merrowlea	D	13-8-63	F	Ch. Malloy of Merrowlea	My Delight of Merrowlea	Mr R. Muir	Capt. & Mrs E.J. Hutton
1968	Try Again of Moonsfield	B	12-3-62	F	Ch. Telton of Moonsfield	Tazana of Moonsfield	Mr & Mrs B.R. Round	Mrs E.M. Harrild
1969	Best Man of Blendon	D	20-11-66	Br	Bridegroom of Blendon	Oonah of Belregis	Miss Osborn & Mrs Birchmore	Mrs O. Bell
1969	Bunyip of Bencaross	B	3-1-66	F	Ch. Oldmanor Pioneer of Daneii	Ch. Try Again of Moonsfield	Mr & Mrs B. Round	Owners
1969	Candy of Walkmyll	B	22-10-65	Br	Ch. Moyalism of Oldmanor	Ch. Walkmyll Moonyean of Edzell	Mrs F.C. Lewis	Mrs F.C. Lewis
1969	Meletalyon of Oldmanor	D	6-12-66	F	Ch. Telaman of Moonsfield	Ch. Meleta of Oldmanor	Rev. & Mrs J.G. Davies	Rev. & Mrs J.G. Davies
1969	Merry Melba of Oldmanor	B	16-1-66	F	Ch. Oldmanor Pioneer of Daneii	Mimelba of Oldmanor	Rev. & Mrs J.G. Davies	Rev. & Mrs J.G. Davies
1969	Myabella of Oldmanor	B	31-5-66	F	Ch. Oldmanor Pioneer of Daneii	Moyahiti of Oldmanor	Mrs M. White	Rev. & Mrs J.G. Davies
1969	Sherelake Storm-Crest of Blendon	D	15-10-64	F	Ch. Benison of Blendon	Sherelake Stormbird	Miss H.M. Osborn	Mr D. Spray
1969	Telera of Moonsfield	B	18-5-65	Br	Ch. Telton of Moonsfield	Neara of Tayntemead	Mrs E.M. Harrild	Mr J. Steel
1970	Fergus of Clausentum	D	28-12-67	F	Clausentum Danelaghs Quillan	Creole of Clausentum	Mrs H.A. & Miss J.M. Lanning	Mrs H.A. & Miss J.M. Lanning

YEAR	NAME	SEX	BIRTH	COL	SIRE	DAM	OWNER	BREEDER
1970	Sarzec Blue Baron	D	3–10–65	Be	Sarzec Blue Saxon	Kana of Kilcroney	Mr & Mrs D. Craig	Mrs E. Walshe & Mrs J. Coyne
1970	My Ambition of Oldmanor	D	25–2–68	F	Ch. Meletalyon of Oldmanor	Missmanor of Oldmanor	Rev. & Mrs J.G. Davies	Rev. & Mrs J.G. Davies
1970	Kaptain of Kilcroney	D	11–5–67	Bk	Ch. Moyalism of Oldmanor	Ir. Ch. Kara of Kilcroney	Mrs G. Le Coyne	Mrs G. Le Coyne
1970	Gowerfield Candy Caress of Aysdaine	B	1–9–67	F	Ch. Oldmanor Pioneer of Daneii	Delilah of Aysdaine	Mr & Mrs A. Clement	Mrs A.B. Shepperd
1970	Miss Monica of Oldmanor	B	24–12–68	F	Ch. Oldmanor Pioneer of Daneii	Miss Bamford of Oldmanor	Rev. & Mrs J.G. Davies	Rev. & Mrs J.G. Davies
1970	Muffettee of Oldmanor	B	18–8–65	F	Ch. Meletalyon of Oldmanor	Missmanor of Oldmanor	Rev. & Mrs J.G. Davies	Rev. & Mrs J.G. Davies
1971	Miss Freedom of Merrowlea	B	1–12–66	F	Ch. Merry Deal of Merrowlea	Miss Carefree of Merrowlea	Mr & Mrs K. Le Mare	Capt. & Mrs E.J. Hutton
1971	Steed of Bringtonhill	D	1–6–68	F	Ch. Telaman of Moonsfield	Solitair of Bringtonhill	Mrs R.W. Ennals	Mrs R.W. Ennals
1971	Gaylaing Astronaut	D	27–2–68	F	Ch. Sherelake Storm Crest of Blendon	Ch. Astrid of Aranton	Mrs J.A. Laing	Owner
1971	Lotus of Walkmyll	B	18–2–69	F	Ch. Bencaross Beau Brummel	Parabar Meriel	Mrs F.C. Lewis	Owner
1971	My Ben of Oldmanor	D	25–2–68	Br	Ch. Oldmanor Pioneer of Daneii	Margery of Oldmanor	Rev. & Mrs J.G. Davies	Owner
1971	Gowerfield Tartan Muse of Moonsfield	B	20–1–68	F	Ch. Telaman of Moonsfield	Tartan of Moonsfield	Mr A. Clements	Mrs E.M. Harrild
1971	Merry Analyst of Oldmanor	D	15–12–68	F	Ch. Meletalyon of Oldmanor	Ch. Merry Melba of Oldmanor	Mr R. Primmer	Rev. & Mrs J.G. Davies
1971	Terrel of Moonsfield	B	13–3–68	F	Ch. Telaman of Moonsfield	Desdamona of Cheluth	Mrs E.M. Harrild	Mr Bellamy
1971	Timelli Caspian	D	11–7–69	F	Ch. Fergus of Clausentum	Timellie Cassandra	Mr & Mrs E.M. Harms-Cooke	Breeder

YEAR	NAME	SEX	BIRTH	COL	SIRE	DAM	OWNER	BREEDER
1971	Mini Artful of Oldmanor	B	17-12-68	F	Ch. Oldmanor Pioneer of Daneii	Minimischief of Oldmanor	Mrs Doyle	Rev. & Mrs J.G. Davies
1971	Leesthorphill Sultan of Escheatlands	D	24-9-68	H	Ch. Surrel of Leesthorphill	Secret of Leesthorphill	Mrs J. Kelly	Dr M. Lloyd
1971	Malindi of Helmlake	B	14-1-70	F	Ch. Fergus of Clausentum	Ch. Miss Freedom of Merrowlea	Mrs K. Le Mare	Breeder
1972	Laburmax Eurydice	B	24-11-68	F	Ch. Oldmanor Pioneer of Daneii	Aliandra of Ancholme	Mr A. Clements	Mrs B.E. Price
1972	Wykendrift Marcellus	D	28-1-70	F	Ch. Gaylaing Astronaut	Radiant Roxanna of Nira	Miss B.E. Boustead	Owner
1972	Simba of Helmlake	D	14-1-70	F	Ch. Fergus of Clausentum	Ch. Miss Freedom of Merrowlea	Mrs K. Le Mare	Owner
1972	Dulcie of Haverdane	B	18-11-68	F	Dominic of Beechfields	Melba Merrie of Oldmanor	Mrs V.N. Forrest	Owner
1973	Impton Duralex Burnita	B	25-4-69	Bk	Nordic Ch. Harmony Hill Lied of Airways	Nordic Ch. Chan-Sonette of Doggline	Mrs M. Everton	Mr & Mrs G. Pettersson
1973	Big Sur of Impton	D	4-5-70	Be	Sarzec Blue Baron	Marpesa of Merrowlea	Mrs M. Everton	Mr & Mrs B. Everton
1973	Merry Muffin of Oldmanor	D	25-11-69	F	Ch. Meletalyon of Oldmanor	Ch. Merry Melba of Oldmanor	Mr & Mrs B. Draper	Rev. & Mrs J.G. Davies
1973	Impton Duralex Bernando	D	25-4-69	Bk	Nordic Ch. Harmony Hill Lied of Airways	Nordic Ch. Chan-Sonette of Doggline	Mrs M. Everton	Mr & Mrs G. Pettersson
1973	Helmlake Mahe	B	24-1-72	F	Simjea's Hamlet	Ch. Miss Freedom of Merrowlea	Mr & Mrs G. Le Mare	Owners
1973	Timellie My Cheerful	B	21-1-71	F	Timellie Cassius	Timellie Cheerful	Mrs E.M. Harms-Cooke	Owner
1973	Walkmyll Kaster of Clausentum	D	20-6-69	F	Ch. Fergus of Clausentum	Jennifer of Clausentum	Mrs F.C. Lewis	Mrs H.A. & Miss J.M. Lanning

YEAR	NAME	SEX	BIRTH	COL	SIRE	DAM	OWNER	BREEDER
1974	Airways Wrangler of Impton	D	30–8–71	Br	Int. & Nordic Ch. Harmony Hill Lied of Airways	Int. & Nordic Ch. Airways Lady Susan	Mr & Mrs B.M. Everton	Mr & Mrs V. Magnusson
1974	Bellote Boffin	D	13–5–71	F	Gulliver of Taftan	Bellote Tendrill of Moonsfield	Mr & Mrs R. McHaffey	Owners
1974	Helmlake Chico	D	5–5–72	H	Helmlake Ben El Eik Vom Forellen-paradies	Helmlake Magic Columbine	Mrs K. Le Mare	Owners
1974	Impton Apache	D	25–11–72	Bk	Nord. & Eng. Ch. Impton Duralex Bernando	Sierra of Impton	Mr & Mrs B.M. Everton	Owners
1974	Sarzec Blue Stewart	D	2–9–68	Be	Sarzec Blue Saxon	Trousseau of Moonsfield	P. Marshall	Mrs E. Walshe
1974	Timellie Cheerleader	D	21–1–71	F	Timellie Cassius	Timellie Cheerful	Mrs V. Harms-Cooke	Owners
1974	Tyegarth Hamlet	D	11–4–69	F	Ch. Meletalyon of Oldmanor	Tyegarth Elsinore	Miss S.F. Cartwright	Owner
1974	Dicarl The Lioness of Jaffrak	B	18–3–73	F	Ch. Simba of Helmlake	Dicarl Tarbaby	Mr & Mrs J. Krall	Mrs D. Johnson
1974	Gracelove Kinda Special	B	28–8–70	F	Gracelove Tinuss of Brookview	Gracelove My Answer of Oldmanor	Mrs & Miss Giles & Mrs Jones	Owners
1974	Helmlake Curieuse	B	24–1–72	F	Simjea's Hamlet	Ch. Miss Freedom of Merrowlea	Mrs K. Le Mare	Owners
1974	Kontiki Coral Reef	B	22–2–71	F	Bucaneer of Beechfields	Kukara of Kontiki	Mr R. Marshall	Owner
1975	Gowerfield Gilden	D	2–9–72	F	Gowerfield Galeforce	Genie of Gowerfield	Mrs A. Heaton	Mr & Mrs A. Clements
1975	Helmlake Praslin	D	24–1–72	Br	Simjea's Hamlet	Ch. Miss Freedom of Merrowlea	Mrs K. Le Mare	Owners
1975	Walkmyll Storm	D	5–11–72	F	Ch. Walkmyll Kaster of Clausentum	Ch. Lotus of Walkmyll	Mrs F.C. Lewis	Owner

YEAR	NAME	SEX	BIRTH	COL	SIRE	DAM	OWNER	BREEDER
1975	Oldmanor Manthem of Auldmoor	B	7-10-72	F	Ch. Meletalyon of Oldmanor	My Design of Oldmanor	Mrs A. Harris	Rev. & Mrs J.G. Davies
1975	Oldmanor Maymirth of Dorneywood	B	31-5-72	F	Ch. Meletalyon of Oldmanor	Ch. Miss Monica of Oldmanor	Mr & Mrs D. Parish	Rev. & Mrs J.G. Davies
1975	Sabuki of Sherain For Bridalane	B	13-8-73	F	Sherain Saul	Gowerfield Garrod	Mrs J. Briggs	M. Griffiths
1975	Shamgret Kosmea	B	4-4-72	F	Robin of Clausentum	Shamgret Fatma Vom Rheinriver	Mr & Mrs W.T. Hale	Owners
1976	Clausentum Gulliver	D	9-3-74	F	Ch. Fergus of Clausentum	Hattie of Clausentum	Mr & Mrs J. Butcher	Mrs & Miss Lanning
1976	Clausentum Magnus	D	18-3-74	F	Ch. Fergus of Clausentum	Hanah of Clausentum	Mrs P.M. Howell & Miss Lanning	Mrs H.A. & Miss J.M. Lanning
1976	Dicarl The Heavyweight	D	3-11-73	F	Gowerfield Galestorm of Aysdaine	Dicarl Tardub	R. Gretton	Mrs D. Johnson
1976	Gowerfield Galestorm of Aysdaine	D	25-7-71	F	Golden Reward of Lisvane	Ch. Gowerfield Tartan Muse of Moonsfield	Mrs A. Sheppard	Mr & Mrs A. Clements
1976	The Weightlifter of Dicarl	D	30-8-75	F	Ch. Dicarl The Heavyweight	Ch. Dicarl The Lioness of Jafrak	Mrs D. Johnson	Mr & Mrs J. Krall
1976	Moonsfield Tellora	B	3-10-73	F	Oakhatch Carl of Moonsfield	Terrell of Moonsfield	Mrs I. Wheeler	Mrs E.M. Harrild
1976	Solveig of Helmlake	B	27-7-73	F	Ch. Simba of Helmlake	Franny of Clausentum	Mr & Mrs G. Le Mare	Mrs L. McCulloch
1976	Dorneywood Dahlia of Walkmyll	B	22-4-75	F	Ch. Walkmyll Storm	Ch. Oldmanor Maymirth of Dorneywood	Mrs F.C. Lewis	Mr & Mrs D. Parish
1976	Beaudan Golden Dawn of Stranahan	B	19-5-74	F	Ch. Bencaross Beau Brummel	Beaudan Tandy	Mr & Mrs C. Tandy	Mr & Mrs J. Reay
1977	Dicarl The Pacemaker of Meadvale	D	19-8-74	F	Dicarl Suprizin Stew	Dicarl Tarbaby	P.F. Stevens	Mrs D. Johnson

YEAR	NAME	SEX	BIRTH	COL	SIRE	DAM	OWNER	BREEDER
1977	Timellie Cinamon	D	1-3-72	F	Ch. Timellie Cheerleader	Timellie Cinlass	Mrs D. McCrindle	Mrs V. Harms-Cooke
1977	Walkmyll Duncan	D	3-6-74	F	Ch. Walkmyll Storm	Tamarisk of Walkmyll	Mrs F.C. Lewis	Owner
1977	Auldmoor Astute	D	9-1-75	F	Int. Nord & Eng. Ch. Airways Wrangler of Impton	Ch. Oldmanor Manthem of of Auldmoor	Mrs N.R. Tilley	Mrs A. Harris
1977	Gracelove Tomorrows Hope	D	23-7-73	Br	Target of Moonsfield	Gracelove Telatone of Moonsfield	Mesdames Giles & Jones and Miss K. Giles	Owners
1977	Bringtonhill Oraya	B	15-9-74	F	Golden Reward of Lisvane	Tawny of Bringtonhill	H.R. Hunt	Mrs R.W. Ennals
1977	Brutondane Delblonde	B	26-3-75	F	Gaylaing Astrolad of Brutondane	Walkmyll Serenade of Brutondane	Mrs J. Alford	Mrs M.A. Roberts
1977	Dunoir Cora	B	4-9-74	H	Ch. Helmlake Chico	Masnou Jacarena of Dunoir	Mrs J.E. Middleton	Owner
1977	Faircrest Easter Wish	B	30-3-75	F	Zeus of Beechfields	Shandiss Sophie of Faircrest	S. Wareing	Mrs J. Cox
1977	Helmlake Fancy Fashion	B	25-7-75	H	Ch. Helmlake Chico	Bettina of Helmlake	Mrs K. Le Mare	Owner
1977	Shamgret Beatrix	B	25-2-75	Br	Shamgret Sascha	Shamgret Dagmar	Mr & Mrs W.T. Hale	Owners
1977	Stranahan Golden Sable of Sallust	B	30-7-73	F	My Hallmark of Oldmanor at Sallust	Beaudan Tanville Lass	Mr & Mrs A.M. Rewston	Mr & Mrs J. Reay
1977	Kontiki Sea Splendour	B	5-8-74	F	Int. Nord & Eng. Ch. Airways Wrangler of Impton	Ch. Kontiki Coral Reef	R. Marshall	Owner
1977	Queen of Carpenders of Vironey	B	6-6-73	F,	Dashtanga Stroller of Bringtonhill	Barnsfield Lady Jane	Mrs V.E. Bishop	J.J. Wiggett
1978	Aysdaine Lion	D	8-10-76	F	Ch. The Weight-lifter of Dicarl	Aysdaine Lightning	Mrs A. Sheppard	Owner

YEAR	NAME	SEX	BIRTH	COL	SIRE	DAM	OWNER	BREEDER
1978	Dicarl The Prizefighter	D	2–8–75	Br	Tresylyan Tudor Minstrel	Dicarl Muffahiti of Oldmanor	Mrs D. Johnson	Owner
1978	Tarus Major Concession	D	7–1–76	F	Tarus Arandyke	Kazim Lisander	Mrs J.A. Wright	Owner
1978	Ulrik of Valkyr	D	4–11–76	Br	Int. Nord & Eng. Ch. Airways Wrangler of Impton	Vitula of Valkyr	Mesdames Williams & Jones	Owners
1978	Dicarl The Hot News	B	28–5–76	F	Ch. Dicarl The Heavyweight	Dicarl Suprizin Stew	Miss L. Robson	Mrs D. Johnson
1978	Dorneywood Debonair	B	23–7–76	F	Ch. Clausentum Gulliver	Ch. Oldmanor Maymirth of Dorneywood	Mr & Mrs D. Parish	Owners
1978	Enydelet Pandora Beauty	B	22–10–73	F	Cantspa Uranus	Historic Lady	Mrs & Mrs J. Taylor	Owners
1978	Halemoss Bettina of Walkmyll	B	28–8–75	F	Ch. Walkmyll Storm	Georlin Deena of Halemoss	Mrs F.C. Lewis	Mrs H. Briscoe
1978	Sherry of Sherain of Salpetra	B	28–7–75	F	Sherain Saul	Gowerfield Garrod	Mr & Mrs P. Anders	Mrs Griffiths
1978	Timellie Clovanna	B	24–10–72	F	Timellie Cassius	Timellie Clover	Mrs V. Harms-Cooke	Owner
1979	Anset Jubilee Boy	D	26–11–76	F	Anset Drum Major	Shamgret Zeta of Anset	Mr & Mrs A. Pearce	Owners
1979	The Contender of Dicarl	D	20–9–77	F	Ch. The Weight-lifter of Dicarl	Endroma Lucky Loo	Mrs D. Johnson	P. Russell
1979	Walkmyll Jaeger	D	5–6–77	F	Danelagh's Eurus of Walkmyll	Ch. Dorneywood Dahlia of Walkmyll	Mrs F.C. Lewis	Owner
1979	Czarina V.T. Buitenburgen of Impton	B	30–6–77	Be	Ch. Impton Apache	Impton Onieda	Mr & Mrs B.M. Everton	Mrs L.E. Van Der Vijver
1979	Dicarl The Dreamseller	B	6–7–77	F	Ch. The Weight-lifter of Dicarl	Dicarl The Croupier	Mrs W.A. Doyle	Mrs D. Johnson

YEAR	NAME	SEX	BIRTH	COL	SIRE	DAM	OWNER	BREEDER
1979	Auldmoor Iolanthe	B	24–12–76	Br	Ch. Walkmyll Storm	Auldmoor Artemis	Mrs A. Harris & Mrs B.R. Tilley	Mrs A. Harris
1979	Jafrak Jungle Stalker of Leebendia	B	30–8–75	F	Ch. Dicarl The Heavyweight	Ch. Dicarl The Lioness of Jafrak	Mr & Mrs C.H. Benjamin	Mr & Mrs J. Krall
1979	Stranahan Shan of Walkmyll	B	26–11–77	F	Danelagh's Eurus of Walkmyll	Ch. Beaudan Golden Dawn of Stranahan	Mrs F.C. Lewis	Mr & Mrs J. Reay
1979	Taranmur Winstons Bell	B	7–1–76	Br	Ch. Gracelove Tomorrows Hope	Timellie Cinova	Mrs G.M. Thorndyke	Owner
1979	The Grandaughter of Dicarl	B	30–8–75	F	Ch. Dicarl The Heavyweight	Ch. Dicarl The Lioness of Jafrak	Mr & Mrs J. Krall	Mrs D. Johnson
1980	Samani Desert Chief	D	16–8–79	F	Lincoln's Winstead Von Raseac	Samani Caprice	Mrs E.M. Bacon	Owner
1980	Dicarl The Hotentot	D	28–5–76	F	Ch. Dicarl The Heavyweight	Dicarl Suprizin Sophie	B.O. Bream & Mrs H.E. Barker	Mrs D. Johnson
1980	Stranahan Shadrak	D	26–11–77	F	Danelagh's Eurus of Walkmyll	Ch. Beaudan Golden Dawn of Stranahan	Mr & Mrs J. Reay	Owners
1980	Talawa of Helmlake of Kilcroney	D	2–2–75	H	Ch. Helmlake Chico	Leslies Taura V. Glenbrae	D.W. Randolph & Mrs G. L'e West-Coyne	Miss Benaim
1980	The Wrestler of Dicarl	D	5–6–77	F	Ch. The Weightlifter of Dicarl	Gaymiles Gorgeous	Mrs S. Verity	Mrs D. Johnson
1980	Vernlam Maxie of Delwin	D	15–6–78	F	Lincoln's Winstead Von Raseac	Sherain Shelagh	Mrs G.A. Goodwin	W. Cowlam
1980	Helmlake Catarina	B	31–3–80	F	Ch. Bellote Boffin	Ch. Helmlake Mahe	Mrs K. Le Mare & Mrs H. Cranham	Mrs K. Le Mare
1980	Dicarl Fancy That	B	14–10–76	F	Ch. Dicarl The Heavyweight	Dicarl The Fancied	Mrs F. Bingham	Mr & Mrs Kirby
1980	Millpark Kreme Kracker	B	7–10–77	F	Warflake Konrad	Millpark Pineapple Poll	Mr & Mrs B. Satterley	Mr & Mrs B. Spurin

YEAR	NAME	SEX	BIRTH	COL	SIRE	DAM	OWNER	BREEDER
1980	Dorneywood Damask	B	23–7–76	F	Ch. Clausentum Gulliver	Ch. Oldmanor Maymirth of Dorneywood	D.R. Bluff	Mr & Mrs D. Parish
1980	Dorneywood Electra	B	23–7–78	F	Danelagh's Eurus of Walkmyll	Ch. Oldmanor Maymirth of Dorneywood	Mr & Mrs D. Parish	Owners
1980	Dorneywood Diorissimo of Drumview	B	23–7–76	F	Ch. Clausentum Gulliver	Ch. Oldmanor Maymirth of Dorneywood	Mrs M. Ramsey	Mr & Mrs D. Parish
1980	Enydelet The Madam	B	31–1–78	F	Ch. The Weight-lifter of Dicarl	Ch. Enydelet Pandora Beauty	Mr & Mrs J. Taylor	Owners
1980	Wilgarie Sza Sza of Salpetra	B	30–8–76	F	Sherain Saul	Gowerfield Garrod	Mr & Mrs P. Anders	Mrs M. Griffiths
1981	Ashville Harvey	D	23–12–75	H	Ch. Helmlake Chico	Ashville Hannah	Mrs A.P. Gillingham	Owner
1981	Dicarl The Interviewer	D	5–4–78	F	Ch. The Weight-lifter of Dicarl	Dicarl The Lady Who	C. Griffiths	Mrs D. Johnson
1981	Helmlake Implicable	D	29–8–78	H	Montego of Helmlake	Ch. Helmlake Fancy Fashion	Mrs K. Le Mare	Owner
1981	Sherain Sheik of Danesworth	D	24–12–77	F	Dorneywood Dandy Lion	Shoona of Sherain	Mrs Alexander	Mrs B. Edmonds
1981	Walkmyll Holly	B	17–5–78	F	Danelagh's Eurus of Walkmyll	Ch. Dorneywood Dahlia of Walkmyll	Mrs F.C. Lewis	Owner
1981	Leenah I'm Mindy	B	11–7–79	F	Walkmyll Oliver of Russara	Coloir The Baroness	Mr & Mrs D.R. Randall	Mrs J. Al-Kudsi
1981	Salpetra Beauful Girl	B	6–6–79	F	Lincoln's Win-stead Von Raseac	Ch. Sherry of Sherain of Salpetra	D. Quinn	Mr & Mrs P. Anders
1981	Stranahan Serendipity	B	26–11–77	F	Danelagh's Eurus of Walkmyll	Ch. Beaudan Golden Dawn of Stranahan	Mr & Mrs J. Reay	Owners
1981	Dicarl Tendellie	B	6–7–79	F	Ch. The Con-tender of Dicarl	Ch. The Gran-daughter of Dicarl	Mr Shaun McAlpine	Mrs Di Johnson

YEAR	NAME	SEX	BIRTH	COL	SIRE	DAM	OWNER	BREEDER
1981	Auldmoor Achaea of Addelos	B	23–10–78	F	Airways Optimist of Impton	Auldmoor Artemis	Mr & Mrs A.D. Howard	Mrs A. Harris
1982	Dicarl The Alliance With Algwynne	D	26–1–81	F	Ch. The Wrestler of Dicarl	Ch. The Gran-daughter of Dicarl	Mr & Mrs A. Herbert	Mrs Di Johnson
1982	Enydelet Super Cool	D	30–9–78	F	Ch. The Weight-lifter of Dicarl	Deansfield Golden Louise	A. Tomlin	Mr & Mrs J. Taylor
1982	Falkenburg Arcas	D	1–9–77	H	Montego of Helmlake	Dicarl Eurika of Falkenburg	Mrs E. Penny	Owner
1982	Walkmyll Faithfull	D	19–9–77	F	Danelagh's Eurus of Walkmyll	Ch. Halemoss Bettina of Walkmyll	Mr & Mrs M. Brown	Mrs F.C. Lewis
1982	The Advocate of Marladane	D	11–9–79	F	Sherain Sauldanti of Marladane	Marladane Sheba	R. Brunning	K. Perera
1982	Jafrak Jinger Cookie	B	5–5–79	F	Ch. The Wrestler of Dicarl	Jafrak Jungle Baby	Mr & Mrs J. Krall	Owners
1982	Daneagle Alexandra	B	19–2–80	F	Archos Angus	Ch. Dorneywood Damask	Mr & Mrs D.R. Bluff	Owners
1982	Daneton Amelia	B	23–4–80	F	Lincoln's Win-stead Von Raseac	Daneton Princess	Mr & Mrs M. Duckworth	Mr & Mrs I.J. Butcher
1982	Drumview Treasure Seeker	B	10–5–79	F	Danelagh's Eurus of Walkmyll	Ch. Dorneywood Diorissimo of Drumview	Mrs M. Ramsey	Owner
1983	Carngray King Solmon of Lismear	D	8–4–80	F	Danelagh's Eurus of Walkmyll	Kohoutek Kalypso	Mrs A. Stephens	Mrs A. Jones
1983	Walkmyll Gregory of Marladane	D	16–4–79	F	Danelagh's Eurus of Walkmyll	Ch. Halemoss Bettina of Walkmyll	Mrs C.A. Jackson	Mrs F.C. Lewis
1983	Yaresville Washington	D	13–10–79	H	Helmlake Gitano	A Black Pearl of Giojan	Mr & Mrs C.A. Cropley	Owners
1983	Tollydane The Tic Tac Man	D	14–2–79	Br	Ch. The Weight-lifter of Dicarl	Branwen of Blendon	Mrs Dunkley	T. Kentish
1983	Dicarl The Guessing Game	B	2–5–80	F	Ch. The Con-tender of Dicarl	Iguesso of Dicarl	R. Holder	Mrs Di Johnson

YEAR	NAME	SEX	BIRTH	COL	SIRE	DAM	OWNER	BREEDER
1983	Dorneywood Infanta of Lismear	B	1–8–81	F	Walkmyll Torquil	Ch. Dorneywood Debonair	Mrs A. Stephens	Mr & Mrs D. Parish
1983	Helmlake Krazy Fashion	B	17–3–80	H	Ch. Helmlake Implicable	Chy An Mor Shin-ing Star of Helmlake	Mrs K. Le Mare	Owner
1983	Hotpoints Fortuna of Walkmyll	B	27–11–80	Br	Int. & Nord. Ch. Gerjos Shilo of Airways	Int. & Nord. Ch. Airways Nebula	Mrs F.C. Lewis	Borghild Sorenson
1983	Impton Motile	B	9–9–80	Be	Gaylord V.T. Buitengebeuren of Impton	Czarina V.T. Buitengebeuren of Impton	Mrs J.M.D. Rice	Mr & Mrs B. Everton
1984	Cid Campeador De Los Madronales of Helmlake	D	28–2–80	F	Span. Ch. Ferro	Span. Ch. Astori De Los Madron-ales	Mrs K. Le Mare	D. Iglesias & D. Del Rio
1984	Devarro Direct Descendant	D	17–1–82	Br	Devarro Director Bains	Dicarl The Autumn of Devarro	Mr & Mrs E. Talbot	Mr & Mrs G. Burton
1984	Lismear Accolade	D	17–1–82	F	Tarus El-Hambra	Tresylyan Corin of Lismear	Mrs A. Stephens	Owner
1984	Picanbil Pericles	D	3–9–81	Br	Ch. Samani Desert Chief	Auldmoor Adella	Miss A. Hartley & Mrs S. Holmes	Owners
1984	Salpetra Silas	D	24–1–81	F	Lincoln's Win-stead Von Raseac	Ch. Wilgarie Sza Sza of Salpetra	Mr & Mrs P. Anders	Owners
1984	Walkmyll Trestarragon	D	8–9–81	F	Danelagh's Helmund of Walkmyll	Ch. Stranahan Shan of Walkmyll	Mrs F.C. Lewis	Owner
1984	Authorpe Hunny-Bear	B	31–12–81	F	The Wizard of Dicarl	Hot Cake of Dicarl	Mrs A.E. Goldthorpe	Owner
1984	Dicarl The Liaison With Algwynne	B	3–12–82	F	Ch. The Con-tender of Dicarl	Baby Grand of Dicarl	Mr & Mrs Les Herbert	Mrs Di Johnson
1984	Arianne of Auldmoor	B	3–9–81	F	Ch. Samani Desert Chief	Auldmoor Adella	Hon. Mrs N. Young	Miss A. Hartley & Mrs S. Holmes
1984	Endroma Black Magic	B	1–7–80	Bk	Gaylord V.T. Buitengebeuren of Impton	Endroma Miss Highlight	Mrs S. MacGowan	Mr & Mrs P. Russell

YEAR	NAME	SEX	BIRTH	COL	SIRE	DAM	OWNER	BREEDER
1984	Dicarl The Lady in Waiting of Jalus	B	2-4-80	F	Ch. The Weightlifter of Dicarl	Dicarl The Lady Who	J. Luscot	Mrs Di Johnson
1985	Yaresville Westminster	D	31-1-83	H	Ch. Yaresville Washington	Yaresville Black Bubbles	Mr & Mrs A. Cropley	Owners
1985	Anset The Smoothie	D	12-7-83	F	Anset Timekeeper	Waterwoods Ballyhoo of Anset	Mr & Mrs A. Pearce	Owners
1985	Walkmyll Montgomery	D	29-8-80	F	Ch. Walkmyll Jaeger	Ch. Stranahan Shan of Walkmyll	Mrs J. Christie	Mrs F. C. Lewis
1985	Devarro Mr Sullivan	D	11-7-83	Br	Devarro Director Bains	Dicarl The Autumn of Devarro	Mr & Mrs T. Botterill	Mr & Mrs G. Burton
1985	Kishmul Cavalier	D	9-10-80	F	Lincoln's Winstead Von Raseac	Maricol Marchioness of Kishmul	Mr & Mrs Macey	Mr & Mrs G. MacNeill
1985	She's Sophie of Dicarl	B	2-2-84	F	Unmistakably of Dicarl	Plain Sailing of Dicarl	Mr & Mrs W. W. Mills	M/s Warwick & Durrant
1985	Dicarl The Crying Time	B	21-9-82	F	The Dicarl Who Waits	I Guess So of Dicarl	M. Simmons	Mrs Di Johnson
1985	Batworth Shanghai Lil	B	16-5-82	Br	Macho Man Sunshine Parkers of Helmlake	Taru of Helmlake and Batworth	Mr Otto & Mr Pakarinen	Owners
1986	Rolling Stone of Dicarl	D	15-7-82	F	The Wrestler of Dicarl	Larkridge Aileen	Mrs M. Phelan	R. S. Woolridge
1986	Airways Eclair of Auldmoor	B	18-9-83	F	Snuggery Cyrano of Airways	Swedish Ch. Airways Ambra	Mrs Ann Foxwell	C.P. & U. Magnusson
1986	Int. & Nord. Ch. Hotpoints New Treasure For Batworth	B	23-12-82	H	Int. Ch. Sonny Boy At Rosenhoi	Int. Ch. French Fashion of Helmlake	M.J. Pakarinen & W. Enger	B. Sorensen
1986	Walkmyll Wonder	D	17-12-82	F	Ch. Walkmyll Trestarragon	Walkmyll Fay	Mr & Mrs R.J. Lovell	Mrs F. C. Lewis
1986	Daneways Dolly Clothes Peg	B	8-9-83	F	Ch. Samani Desert Chief	Daneways Dolly Daydream	Doyle	Owners
1986	Yacanto Tudor Melody	B	7-7-82	Br	Ch. Samani Desert Chief	Chapala Dixie Pixie of Yacanto	Mr & Mrs M. R. Bousefield and Mrs P. Busby	Mr and Mrs M.R. Bousefield

YEAR	NAME	SEX	BIRTH	COL	SIRE	DAM	OWNER	BREEDER
1986	Aristocrat of Daneton	D	27-12-83	F	Ch. Samani Desert Chief	Daneton Francesca	Mrs M. Armstrong	Mrs M. Armstrong
1986	Smooth Sailing of Dicarl	B	23-9-84	F	Unmistakably of Dicarl	Plain Sailing of Dicarl	Mrs Di Johnson	M/s Warwick & Durrant
1986	Helmlake Next In Line	D	13-2-84	H	Ch. Helmlake Implicable	Chyanmor Lovely Lady of Tarus	Mrs K. Le Mare	Mrs K. Le Mare

Appendix VI

Great Dane Breed Clubs

1 *The Midland & West Of England Great Dane Club*
Hon. Secretary . . . Mrs Sylvia Burton
Russetways, 167 Mansfield Road, Papplewick, Nottingham.

2 *The Great Dane Club*
Hon. Secretary . . . Mrs Freda Lewis
Lodge Farm, Bridgtown, Cannock, Staffs.

3 *Great Dane Breeders' Association*
Hon. Secretary . . . Mrs Marie Stevens
'Highfield', Longfield Avenue, New Barn, Dartford, Kent.

4 *The Northern Great Dane Club*
Hon. Secretary . . . Mr Ben Round
'Larkhill', Moorend, Mellor, Nr. Stockport, SK6 SP5.

5 *South Western Great Dane Club*
Hon. Secretary . . . Mr W. Spurin
Mill Park, Cardinham, Bodmin, Cornwall.

6 *East Of England Great Dane Club*
Hon. Secretary . . . Miss B.E. Boustead
Wyke Farm, Mileham, Kings Lynn, Norfolk.

7 *Pennine Great Dane Club*
Hon. Secretary . . . Mrs S. Yule
10 Front Street, Broompark, Durham, DH7 7QX.

8 *The Great Dane Club Of South Wales*
Hon. Secretary . . . Mrs M. Jeffries
2 Price Avenue, Barry, South Glamorgan, CF6 7JR.

9 *The Scottish Great Dane Club*
Hon. Secretary . . . Mrs J. Christie
The Gables, Bellevue Avenue, Kirkintilloch, Glasgow, G66 1AJ.

Index